T0143816

The Book of
All-Power

The Book of All-Power

Edgar Wallace

MINT EDITIONS

The Book of All-Power was first published in 1921.

This edition published by Mint Editions 2020.

ISBN 9781513220222 | E-ISBN 9781513266855

Published by Mint Editions®

MINT
EDITIONS

minteditionbooks.com

Publishing Director: Jennifer Newens
Project Manager: Gabrielle Maudiere
Design & Production: Rachel Lopez Metzger
Typesetting: Westchester Publishing Services

Contents

Chapter 1

Introducing Malcolm Hay

If a man is not eager for adventure at the age of twenty-two, the enticement of romantic possibilities will never come to him.

The chairman of the Ukraine Oil Company looked with a little amusement at the young man who sat on the edge of a chair by the chairman's desk, and noted how the eye of the youth had kindled at every fresh discouragement which the chairman had put forward. Enthusiasm, reflected the elder man, was one of the qualities which were most desirable in the man who was to accept the position which Malcolm Hay was at that moment considering.

"Russia is a strange country," said Mr. Tremayne. "It is one of the mystery places of the world. You hear fellows coming back from China who tell you amazing stories of the idiosyncrasies of the Chink. But I can tell you, from my own personal observations, that the Chinaman is an open book in words of one syllable compared with the average Russian peasant. By the way, you speak Russian, I understand?"

Hay nodded.

"Oh, yes, sir," he said, "I have been talking Russian ever since I was sixteen, and I speak both the dialects."

"Good!" nodded Mr. Tremayne. "Now, all that remains for you to do is to think both dialects. I was in Southern Russia attending to our wells for twenty years. In fact, long before our wells came into being, and I can honestly say that, though I am not by any means an unintelligent man, I know just as little about the Russian to-day as I did when I went there. He's the most elusive creature. You think you know him two days after you have met him. Two days later you find that you have changed all your opinions about him; and by the end of the first year, if you have kept a careful note of your observations and impressions in a diary, you will discover that you have three hundred and sixty-five different views—unless it happens to be a leap year."

"What happens in a leap year?" asked the innocent Hay.

"You have three hundred and sixty-six views," said the solemn Mr. Tremayne.

He struck a bell.

"We shan't want you to leave London for a week or two," he said, "and in the meantime you had better study up our own special literature. We can give you particulars about the country—that part of the country in which the wells are situated—which you will not find in the guidebooks. There are also a few notable personages whom it will be advisable for you to study."

"I know most of them," said the youth with easy confidence. "As a matter of fact, I got the British Consul to send me a local directory and swotted it."

Mr. Tremayne concealed a smile.

"And what did the local directory say about Israel Kensky?" he asked innocently.

"Israel Kensky?" said the puzzled youth. "I don't remember that name."

"It is the only name worth remembering," said the other dryly, "and, by the way, you'll be able to study him in a strange environment, for he is in London at this moment."

A clerk had answered the bell and stood waiting in the doorway.

"Get Mr. Hay those books and pamphlets I spoke to you about," said Tremayne. "And, by the way, when did M. Kensky arrive?"

"To-day," said the clerk.

Tremayne nodded.

"In fact," he said, "London this week will be filled with people whose names are not in your precious directory, and all of whom you should know. The Yaroslavs are paying a sort of state visit."

"The Yaroslavs?" repeated Hay. "Oh, of course——"

"The Grand Duke and his daughter," added Mr. Tremayne.

"Well," smiled the young man, "I'm not likely to meet the Grand Duke or the Grand Duchess. I understand the royal family of Russia is a little exclusive."

"Everything is likely in Russia," said the optimistic Mr. Tremayne. "If you come back in a few years' time and tell me that you've been appointed an admiral in the Russian Navy, or that you've married the Grand Duchess Irene Yaroslav, I shall not for one moment disbelieve you. At the same time, if you come back from Russia without your ears, the same having been cut off by your peasant neighbours to propitiate the ghost of a martyr who died six hundred years ago, I shall not be surprised either. That is the country you're going to—and I envy you."

"I'm a little surprised at myself," admitted Malcolm, "it seems almost incredible. Of course, sir, I have a lot to learn and I'm not placing too much reliance upon my degree."

"Your science degree?" said Tremayne. "It may be useful, but a divinity degree would have been better."

"A divinity degree?"

Tremayne nodded.

"It is religion you want in Russia, and especially local religion. You'll have to do a mighty lot of adapting when you're out there, Hay, and I don't think you could do better than get acquainted with the local saints. You'll find that the birth or death of four or five of them are celebrated every week, and that your workmen will take a day's holiday for each commemoration. If you're not pretty smart, they'll whip in a few saints who have no existence, and you'll get no work done at all—that will do."

He ended the interview with a jerk of his head, and as the young man got to his feet to go, added: "Come back again to-morrow. I think you ought to see Kensky."

"Who is he?" asked Hay courteously. "A local magnate?"

"In a sense he is and in a sense he's not," said the careful Mr. Tremayne. "He's a big man locally, and from a business point of view, I suppose he is a magnate. However, you'll be able to judge for yourself."

Malcolm Hay went out into the teeming streets of London, walking on air. It was his first appointment—he was earning money, and it seemed rather like a high-class dream.

In Maida Vale there are many little side streets, composed of shabby houses covered with discoloured stucco, made all the more desolate and gloomy in appearance by the long and narrow strip of "garden" which runs out to the street. In one of these, devoted to the business of a boarding-house, an old man sat at a portable bench, under the one electric light which the economical landlady had allowed him. The room was furnished in a typically boarding-house style.

But both the worker at the bench, and the woman who sat by the table, her chin on her palms, watching him, seemed unaffected by the poverty of their surroundings. The man was thin and bent of back. As he crouched over the bench, working with the fine tools on what was evidently intended to be the leather cover of a book, his face lay in the shadow, and only the end of his straggling white beard betrayed his age.

Presently he looked up at the woman and revealed himself as a hawk-nosed man of sixty. His face was emaciated and seamed, and his dark eyes shone brightly. His companion was a woman of twenty-four, obviously of the Jewish type, as was the old man; what good looks she possessed were marred by the sneer on her lips.

"If these English people see you at work," she said presently, "they will think you are some poor man, little father."

Israel Kensky did not stop his work.

"What book are you binding?" she asked after awhile. "Is it the Talmud which Levi Leviski gave you?"

The old man did not answer, and a dark frown gathered on the woman's heavy face. You might not guess that they were father and daughter, yet such was the case. But between Sophia Kensky and her father there was neither communion of spirit nor friendship. It was amazing that she should accompany him, as she did, wherever he went, or that he should be content to have her as his companion. The gossips of Kieff had it that neither would trust the other out of sight; and it may be that there was something in this, though a stronger motive might be suspected in so far as Sophia's actions were concerned.

Presently the old man put down his tools, blinked, and pushed back his chair.

"It is a design for a great book," he said, and chuckled hoarsely. "A book with steel covers and wonderful pages." He smiled contemptuously. "The Book of All-Power," he said.

"Little father, there are times when I think you are mad. For how can you know the secrets which are denied to others? And you who write so badly, how can you fill a great book with your writings?"

"The Book of All-Power," repeated the man, and the smile on the woman's face grew broader.

"A wonderful book!" she scoffed, "filled with magic and mystery and spells—do you wonder that we of Kieff suspect you?"

"We of Kieff?" he repeated mockingly, and she nodded.

"We of Kieff," she said.

"So you are with the rabble, Sophia!" He lifted one shoulder in a contemptuous little gesture.

"You are also of the rabble, Israel Kensky," she said. "Do you take your dinner in the Grand Duke's palace?"

He was gathering together the tools on the table, and methodically fitting each graver into a big leather purse.

"The Grand Duke does not stone me in the street, nor set fire to my houses," he said.

"Nor the Grand Duchess," said the girl meaningly, and he looked at her from under his lowered brows.

"The Grand Duchess is beyond the understanding of such as you," he said harshly, and the woman laughed.

"There will come a day when she will be on her knees to me," she said prophetically, and she got up from the table with a heavy yawn. "That I promise myself, and with this promise I put myself to sleep every night."

She went on and she spoke without heat.

"I see her sweeping my floors and eating the bread I throw to her."

Israel Kensky had heard all this before, and did not even smile.

"You are an evil woman, Sophia," he said. "God knows how such a one could be a daughter of mine. What has the Grand Duchess done to you that you should harbour such venom?"

"I hate her because she is," said the woman evenly. "I hate her not for the harm she has done me, but for the proud smile she gives to her slaves. I hate her because she is high and I am low, and because all the time she is marking the difference between us."

"You are a fool," said Israel Kensky as he left the room.

"Perhaps I am," said the woman, his daughter. "Are you going to bed now?"

He turned in the doorway.

"I am going to my room. I shall not come down again," he said.

"Then I will sleep," she yawned prodigiously. "I hate this town."

"Why did you come?" he asked. "I did not want you."

"I came because you did not want me," said Sophia Kensky.

Israel went to his room, closed the door and locked it. He listened and presently he heard the sound of his daughter's door close also and heard the snap of the key as it turned. But it was a double snap, and he knew that the sound was intended for him and that the second click was the unlocking of the door. She had locked and unlocked it in one motion. He waited, sitting in an arm-chair before a small fire, for ten minutes, and then, rising, crossed the room softly and switched out the light. There was a transom above the door, so that anybody in the passage outside could tell whether his light was on or off. Then he resumed his seat, spreading his veined hands to the fire, and listened.

He waited another quarter of an hour before he heard a soft creak and the sound of breathing outside the door. Somebody was standing there listening. The old man kept his eyes fixed on the fire, but his senses were alive to every sound. Again he heard the creaking, this time louder.

A jerry-built house in Maida Vale does not offer the best assistance to the furtive business in which Sophia Kensky was engaged. Another creak, this time farther away and repeated at intervals, told him that she was going down the stairs. He walked to the window and gently pulled up the blind, taking his station so that he could command a view of the narrow strip of garden. Presently his vigil was rewarded. He saw her dark figure walk along the flagged pavement, open the gate and disappear into the darkened street.

Israel Kensky went back to his chair, stirred the fire and settled down to a long wait, his lined face grave and anxious.

The woman had turned to the right and had walked swiftly to the end of the street. The name of that street, or its pronunciation, were beyond her. She neither spoke English, nor was she acquainted with the topography of the district in which she found herself. She slowed her pace as she reached the main road and a man came out of the shadows to meet her.

"Is it you, little mother?" he asked in Russian.

"Thank God you're here! Who is this?" asked Sophia breathlessly.

"Boris Yakoff," said the other, "I have been waiting for an hour, and it is very cold."

"I could not get away before," she said as she fell in beside him. "The old man was working with his foolery and it was impossible to get him to go to bed. Once or twice I yawned, but he took no notice."

"Why has he come to London?" asked her companion. "It must be something important to bring him away from his money-bags."

To this the woman made no reply. Presently she asked:

"Do we walk? Is there no droski or little carriage?"

"Have patience, have patience!" grinned the man good humouredly. "Here in London we do things in grand style. We have an auto-car for you. But it was not wise to bring it so close to your house, little mother. The old man——"

"Oh, finish with the old man," she said impatiently; "do not forget that I am with him all the day."

The antipathy between father and daughter was so well known that the man made no apology for discussing the relationship with that frankness which is characteristic of the Russian peasant. Nor did Sophia Kensky resent the questions of a stranger, nor hesitate to unburden herself of her grievances. The "auto-car" proved to be a very commonplace taxi-cab, though a vehicle of some luxury to Yakoff.

"They say he practises magic," said that garrulous man, as the taxi got on its way; "also that he bewitches you."

"That is a lie," said the woman indifferently: "he frightens me sometimes, but that is because I have here"—she tapped her forehead—"a memory which is not a memory. I seem to remember something just at the end of a thread, and I reach for it, and lo! it is gone!"

"That is magic," said Yakoff gravely. "Evidently he practises his spells upon you. Tell me, Sophia Kensky, is it true that you Jews use the blood of Christian children for your beastly ceremonies?"

The woman laughed.

"What sort of man are you that you believe such things?" she asked contemptuously. "I thought all the comrades in London were educated?"

Yakoff made a little clicking noise with his mouth to betray his annoyance. And well he might resent this reflection upon his education, for he held a university degree and had translated six revolutionary Russian novels into English and French. This, he explained with some detail, and the girl listened with little interest. She was not surprised that an educated man should believe the fable of human sacrifices, which had gained a certain currency in Russia. Only it seemed to her just a little inexplicable.

The cab turned out of the semi-obscurity of the side street into a brilliantly lighted thoroughfare and bowled down a broad and busy road. A drizzle of rain was falling and blurred the glass; but even had the windows been open, she could not have identified her whereabouts.

"To what place are you taking me?" she asked. "Where is the meeting?"

Yakoff lowered his voice to a husky whisper.

"It is the café of the Silver Lion, in a place called Soho," he said. "Here we meet from day to day and dream of a free Russia. We also play bagatelle." He gave the English name for the latter. "It is a club and a restaurant. To-night it is necessary that you should be here, Sophia Kensky, because of the great happenings which must follow."

She was silent for a while, then she asked whether it was safe, and he laughed.

"Safe!" he scoffed. "There are no secret police in London. This is a free country, where one may do as one wishes. No, no, Sophia Kensky, be not afraid."

"I am not afraid," she answered, "but tell me, Yakoff, what is this great meeting about?"

"You shall learn, you shall learn, little sister," said Yakoff importantly.

He might have added that he also was to learn, for as yet he was in ignorance.

They drove into a labyrinth of narrow streets and stopped suddenly before a doorway. There was no sign of a restaurant, and Yakoff explained, before he got out of the cab, that this was the back entrance to the Silver Lion, and that most of the brethren who used the club also used this back door.

He dismissed the cab and pressed a bell in the lintel of the door. Presently it was opened and they passed in unchallenged. They were in a small hallway, lighted with a gas-jet. There was a stairway leading to the upper part of the premises, and a narrower stairway, also lighted by gas, at the foot leading to the cellar; and it was down the latter that Yakoff moved, followed by the girl.

They were now in another passage, whitewashed and very orderly. A gas-jet lit this also, and at one end the girl saw a plain, wooden door. To this Yakoff advanced and knocked. A small wicket, set in the panel, was pushed aside, and after a brief scrutiny by the door's custodian, it was opened and the two entered without further parley.

Chapter 2

A Gun-Man Refuses Work

It was a big underground room, the sort of basement dining-room one finds in certain of the cafés in Soho, and its decorations and furniture were solid and comfortable. There were a dozen men in this innocent-looking saloon when the girl entered. They were standing about talking, or sitting at the tables playing games. The air was blue with tobacco smoke.

Her arrival seemed to be the signal for the beginning of a conference. Four small tables were drawn from the sides and placed together, and in a few seconds she found herself one of a dozen that sat about the board.

The man who seemed to take charge of the proceedings she did not know. He was a Russian—a big, clean-shaven man, quietly and even well-dressed. His hair was flaming red, his nose was crooked. It was this crooked nose which gave her a clue to his identity. She remembered in Kieff, where physical peculiarities could not pass unnoticed, some reference to "twist nose," and racked her brains in an effort to recall who that personage was. That he knew her he very quickly showed.

"Sophia Kensky," he said, "we have sent for you to ask you why your father is in London."

"If you know my father," she replied, "you know also that I, his daughter, do not share his secrets."

The man at the head of the table nodded.

"I know him," he said grimly, "also I know you, Sophia. I have seen you often at the meetings of our society in Kieff."

Again she frowned, trying to recall his name and where she had seen him. It was not at any of the meetings of the secret society—of that she was sure. He seemed to read her thoughts, for he laughed—a deep, thunderous laugh which filled the underground room with sound.

"It is strange that you do not know me," he said, "and yet I have seen you a hundred times, and you have seen me."

A light dawned on her.

"Boolba, the *buffet-schek* of the Grand Duke!" she gasped.

He nodded, absurdly pleased at the recognition.

"I do not attend the meetings in Kieff, little sister, for reasons which you will understand. But here in London, where I have come in advance of Yaroslav, it is possible. Now, Sophia Kensky, you are a proved friend of our movement?"

She nodded, since the statement was in the way of a question.

"It is known to you, as to us, that your father, Israel Kensky, is a friend of the Grand Duchess."

Boolba, the President, saw the sullen look on her face and drew his own conclusions, even before she explained her antipathy to the young girl who held that exalted position.

"It is a mystery to me, Boolba," she said, "for what interest can this great lady have in an old Jew?"

"The old Jew is rich," said Boolba significantly.

"So also is Irene Yaroslav," said the girl. "It is not for money that she comes."

"It is not for money," agreed the other, "it is for something else. When the Grand Duchess Irene was a child, she was in the streets of Kieff one day in charge of her nurse. It happened that some Caucasian soldiers stationed in the town started a pogrom against the Jews. The soldiers were very drunk; they were darting to and fro in the street on their little horses, and the nurse became frightened and left the child. Your father was in hiding, and the soldiers were searching for him; yet, when he saw the danger of the Grand Duchess, he ran from his hiding-place, snatched her up under the hoofs of the horses, and bore her away into his house."

"I did not know this," said Sophia, listening open-mouthed. Her father had never spoken of the incident, and the curious affection which this high-born lady had for the old usurer of Kieff had ever been a source of wonder to her.

"You know it now," said Boolba. "The Grand Duke has long since forgotten what he owes to Israel Kensky, but the Grand Duchess has not. Therefore, she comes to him with all her troubles—and that, Sophia Kensky, is why we have sent for you."

There was a silence.

"I see," she said at last, "you wish me to spy upon Israel Kensky and tell you all that happens."

"I want to know all that passes between him and the Grand Duchess," said Boolba. "She comes to London to-morrow with her father, and it is certain she will seek out Israel Kensky. Every letter that passes between them must be opened."

"But——" she began.

"There is no 'but,'" roared Boolba. "Hear and obey; it is ordered!"

He turned abruptly to the man on his left.

"You understand, Yaroslav arrives in London to-morrow. It is desirable that he should not go away."

"But, but, Excellency," stammered the man on his left, "here in London!"

Boolba nodded.

"But, Excellency," wailed the man, "in London we are safe; it is the one refuge to which our friends can come. If such a thing should happen, what would be our fate? We could not meet together. We should be hounded down by the police from morning until night; we should be deported—it would be the ruin of the great movement."

"Nevertheless, it is an order," said Boolba doggedly; "this is a matter beyond the cause. It will gain us powerful protectors at the court, and I promise you that, though the commotion will be great, yet it will not last for very long, and you will be left undisturbed."

"But——" began one of the audience, and Boolba silenced him with a gesture.

"I promise that none of you shall come to harm, my little pigeons, and that you shall not be concerned in this matter."

"But who will do it, Excellency?" asked another member.

"That is too important to be decided without a meeting of all the brethren. For my part, I would not carry out such an order unless I received the instructions of our President."

"I promise that none of you shall take a risk," sneered Boolba. "Now speak, Yakoff!"

The man who had accompanied Sophia Kensky smiled importantly at the company, then turned to Sophia.

"Must I say this before Sophia Kensky?" he asked.

"Speak," said Boolba. "We are all brothers and sisters, and none will betray you."

Yakoff cleared his throat.

"When your Excellency wrote to me from Kieff, asking me to find a man, I was in despair," he began—an evidently rehearsed speech, "I tore my hair, I wept——"

"Tell us what you have done," said the impatient Boolba. "For what does it matter, in the name of the saints and the holy martyrs" (everyone at the table, including Boolba, crossed himself) "whether your hair was torn or your head was hammered?"

"It was a difficult task, Excellency," said Yakoff in a more subdued tone, "but Providence helped me. There is a good comrade of ours who is engaged in punishing the bourgeoisie by relieving them of their goods——"

"A thief, yes," said Boolba.

"Through him I learnt that a certain man had arrived in England and was in hiding. This man is a professional assassin."

They looked at him incredulously, all except Boolba, who had heard the story before.

"An assassin?" said one. "Of what nationality?"

"American," said Yakoff, and there was a little titter of laughter.

"It is true," interrupted Boolba. "This man, whom Yakoff has found, is what is known in New York as a gun-man. He belongs to a gang which was hunted down by the police, and our comrade escaped."

"But an American!" persisted one of the unconvinced.

"An American," said Yakoff. "This man is desired by the police on this side, and went in hiding with our other comrade, who recognized him."

"A gun-man," said Boolba thoughtfully, and he used the English word with some awkwardness. "A gun-man. If he would only—is he here?" he demanded, looking up.

Yakoff nodded.

"Does he know——"

"I have told him nothing, Excellency," said Yakoff, rising from the table with alacrity, "except to be here, near the entrance to the club, at this hour. Shall I bring him down?"

Boolba nodded, and three minutes later, into this queer assembly, something of a fish out of water and wholly out of his element, strode Cherry Bim, that redoubtable man.

He was a little, man, stoutly built and meanly dressed. He had a fat, good-humoured face and a slight moustache, and eyes that seemed laughing all the time.

Despite the coldness of the night, he wore no waistcoat, and as a protest against the conventions he had dispensed with a collar. As he stood there, belted about his large waist, a billycock hat on the back of his head, he looked to be anything from a broken-down publican to an out-of-work plumber.

He certainly did not bear the impress of gun-man.

If he was out of his element, he was certainly not out of conceit with himself. He gave a cheery little nod to every face that was turned to him, and stood, his hands thrust through his belt, his legs wide apart, surveying the company with a benevolent smile.

"Good evening, ladies and gents," he said. "Shake hands with Cherry Bim! Bim on my father's side and Cherry by christening—Cherry Bim, named after the angels." And he beamed again.

This little speech, delivered in English, was unintelligible to the majority of those present, including Sophia Kensky, but Yakoff translated it. Solemnly he made a circuit of the company and as solemnly shook hands with every individual, and at last he came to Boolba; and only then did he hesitate for a second.

Perhaps in that meeting there came to him some premonition of the future, some half-revealed, half-blurred picture of prophecy. Perhaps that picture was one of himself, lying in the darkness on the roof of the railway carriage, and an obscene Boolba standing erect in a motor-car on the darkened station, waving his rage, ere the three quick shots rang out.

Cherry Bim confessed afterwards to a curious shivery sensation at his spine. The hesitation was only for a second, and then his hand gripped the big hand of the self-constituted chairman.

"Now, gents and ladies," he said, with a comical little bow towards Sophia, "I understand you're all good sports here, and I'm telling you that I don't want to stay long. I'm down and out, and I'm free to confess it, and any of you ladies and gents who would like to grubstake a stranger in a foreign land, why, here's your chance. I'm open to take on any kind of job that doesn't bring me into conspicuous relationship with the bulls—bulls, ladies and gentlemen, being New York for policemen."

Then Boolba spoke, and he spoke in English, slow but correct.

"Comrade," he said, "do you hate tyrants?"

"If he's a copper," replied Mr. Bim mistakenly. "Why, he's just as popular with me as a hollow tooth at an ice-cream party."

"What does he say?" asked the bewildered Boolba, who could not follow the easy flow of Mr. Bim's conversation, and Yakoff translated to the best of his ability.

And then Boolba, arresting the interruption of the American, explained. It was a long explanation. It dealt with tyranny and oppression and other blessed words dear to the heart of the revolutionary; it concerned millions of men and hundreds of millions of men and women in chains, under iron heels, and the like; and Mr. Bim grew more and more hazy, for he was not used to the parabole, the allegory, or the metaphor. But towards the end of his address, Boolba became more explicit, and, as his emotions were moved, his English a little more broken.

Mr. Bim became grave, for there was no mistaking the task which had been set him.

"Hold hard, mister," he said. "Let's get this thing right. There's a guy you want to croak. Do I get you right?"

Again Mr. Yakoff translated the idioms, for Yakoff had not lived on the edge of New York's underworld without acquiring some knowledge of its language.

Boolba nodded.

"We desire him killed," he said. "He is a tyrant, an oppressor——"

"Hold hard," said Bim. "I want to see this thing plain. You're going to croak this guy, and I'm the man to do it? Do I get you?"

"That is what I desire," said Boolba, and Bim shook his head.

"It can't be done," he said. "I'm over here for a quiet, peaceful life, and anyway, I've got nothing on this fellow. I'm not over here to get my picture in the papers. It's a new land to me—why, if you put me in Piccadilly Circus I shouldn't know which way to turn to get out of it! Anyway, that strong arm stuff is out so far as I'm concerned."

"What does he say?" said Boolba again, and again Yakoff translated.

"I thought you were what you call a gun-man," said Boolba with a curl of his lip. "I did not expect you to be frightened."

"There's gun-men and gun-men," said Cherry Bim, unperturbed by the patent sarcasm. "And then there's me. I never drew a gun on a man in my life that didn't ask for it, or in the way of business. No, sirree. You can't hire Cherry Bim to do a low, vulgar murder."

His tone was uncompromising and definite. Boolba realized that he could not pursue his argument with any profit to himself, and that if he were to bring this unwilling agent to his way of thinking a new line would have to be taken.

"You will not be asked to take a risk for nothing," he said. "I am authorized to pay you twenty thousand roubles, that is, two thousand pounds in your money——"

"Not mine," interrupted Bim. "It's ten thousand dollars you're trying to say. Well, even that doesn't tempt me. It's not my game, anyway," he said, pulling up a chair and sitting down in the most friendly manner. "And don't think you're being original when you offer me this commission. I've had it offered me before in New York City, and I've always turned it down, though I know my way to safety blindfolded. That's all there is to it, gentlemen—and ladies," he added.

"So you refuse?" Neither Boolba's voice nor his manner was pleasant.

"That's about the size of it," said Cherry Bim, rising. "I'm a grafter, I admit it. There ain't hardly anything I wouldn't do from smashing a bank downwards, to turn a dishonest penny. But, gents, I'm short of the necessary nerve, inclination, lack of morals, and general ungodliness, to take on murder in the first, second, or third degree."

"You have courage, my friend," said Boolba significantly. "You do not suppose we should take you into our confidence and let you go away again so easily?"

Mr. Bim's smile became broader.

"Gents, I won't deceive you," he said. "I expected a rough house and prepared for it. Watch me!"

He extended one of his hands in the manner of a conjurer and with the other pulled up the sleeve above the wrist. He turned the hands over, waggling the fingers as though he were giving a performance, and they watched him curiously.

"There's nothing there, is there?" said Cherry Bim, beaming at the company, "and yet there is something there. Look!"

No eyes were sharp enough to follow the quick movement of his hand. None saw it drop or rise again. There was a slur of movement, and then, in the hand which had been empty, was a long-barrelled Colt. Cherry Bim, taking no notice of the sensation he created, tossed the revolver to the ceiling and caught it again.

"Now, gents, I don't know whether you're foolish or only just crazy. Get away from that door, Hector," he said to a long-haired man who stood with folded arms against the closed door. And "Hector," whose name was Nickolo Novoski Yasserdernski in real life, made haste to obey.

"Wait a bit," said the careful gun-man. "That's a key in your waistcoat pocket, I guess." He thrust the barrel of his revolver against the other's side, and the long-haired man doubled up with a gasp. But Cherry Bim meant no mischief. The barrel of the gun clicked against the end of a key, and when Cherry Bim drew his revolver away the key was hanging to it!

"Magnetic," the gun-man kindly explained; "it is a whim of mine."

With no other words he passed through the door and slammed it behind him.

Chapter 3

THE GRAND DUCHESS IRENE

Israel Kensky was dozing before the fire when the sound of the creaking stair woke him. He walked softly to the door and listened, and presently he heard the steps of his daughter passing along the corridor. He opened the door suddenly and stepped out, and she jumped back with a little cry of alarm. There were moments when she was terribly afraid of her father, and such a moment came to her now.

"Are you not asleep, Israel Kensky?" she faltered.

"I could not sleep," replied the other, in so mild a tone that she took courage. "Come into my room. I wish to speak to you."

He did not ask her where she had been, or to explain why, at three o'clock in the morning, she was dressed for the street, and she felt it necessary to offer some explanation.

"You wonder why I am dressed?" she said.

"I heard a great noise in the street, and went out to see——"

"What does it matter?" said Israel Kensky. "Save your breath, little daughter. Why should you not walk in the street if you desire?"

He switched on the light to augment the red glow which came from the fire.

"Sit down, Sophia," he said, "I have been waiting for you. I heard you go out."

She made no reply. There was fear in her eyes, and all the time she was conscious of many unpleasant interviews with her father—interviews which had taken place in Kieff and in other towns—the details of which she could never recall. And she was filled with a dread of some happening to which she could not give form or description. He saw her shifting in her chair and smiled slowly.

"Get me the little box which is on my dressing-table, Sophia Kensky," he said.

He was seated by the fire, his hands outstretched to the red coal. After a moment's hesitation she got up, went to the dressing-table, and brought back a small box. It was heavy and made of some metal over which a brilliant black enamel had been laid.

"Open the box, Sophia Kensky," said the old man, not turning his head.

She had a dim recollection that she had been asked to do this before, but again could not remember when or in what circumstances. She opened the lid and looked within. On a bed of black velvet was a tiny convex mirror, about the size of a sixpence. She looked at this, and was still looking at it when she walked slowly back to her chair and sat down. It had such a fascination, this little mirror, that she could not tear her eyes away.

"Close your eyes," said Kensky in a monotonous voice, and she obeyed. "You cannot open them," said the old man, and she shook her head and repeated:

"I cannot open them."

"Now you shall tell me, Sophia Kensky, where you went this night."

In halting tones she told him of her meeting with Yakoff, of their walk, of the cab, of the little door in the back street, and the stone stairs that led to the whitewashed passage; and then she gave, as near as she knew, a full account of all that had taken place. Only when she came to describe Bim and to tell of what he said, did she flounder. Bim had spoken in a foreign language, and the translation of Yakoff had conveyed very little to her. But in this part of the narrative the old man was less interested. Again and again he returned to Boolba and the plot.

"What hand will kill the Grand Duke?" he asked, not once but many times, and invariably she answered:

"I do not know."

"On whose behalf does Boolba act?" asked the old man. "Think, Sophia Kensky! Who will give this foreigner twenty thousand roubles?"

"I do not know," she answered again.

Presently a note of distress was evident in her voice, and Israel Kensky rose up and took the box from her hand.

"You will go to bed, Sophia Kensky," he said slowly and deliberately, "and to-morrow morning, when you wake, you shall not remember anything that happened after you came into this house to-night. You shall not remember that I spoke to you or that I asked you to look in the little box. Do you understand?"

"Yes, Israel Kensky," she replied slowly, and walked with weary feet from the room.

Israel Kensky listened and heard her door click, then closed his own, and, sitting at a table, began to write quickly. He was still writing when the grey dawn showed in his windows at six o'clock. He blotted the last letter and addressed an envelope to "The Most Excellent and Illustrious

Highness the Grand Duchess Irene Yaroslav" before, without troubling to undress, he sank down upon his bed into a sleep of exhaustion.

Malcolm Hay had an appointment with Mr. Tremayne on the morning that saw Israel Kensky engaged in frantic letter-writing. It was about Kensky that Tremayne spoke.

"He has arrived in London," he said, "and is staying in Colbury Terrace, Maida Vale. I think you had better see him, because, as I told you, he is a local big-wig and may be very useful to you. Our wells, as you know, are about thirty miles outside Kieff, which is the nearest big town, so you may be seeing him pretty often. Also, by the way, he is our agent. If you have any trouble with Government officials you must see Kensky, who can generally put things square."

"I believe his daughter is with him," Mr. Tremayne went on, "but I know very little about her. Yet another neighbour of yours arrives by special train at midday."

"Another neighbour of mine?" repeated Malcolm with a smile. "And who is that?"

"The Grand Duke Yaroslav. I don't suppose you'll have very much to do with him, but he's the King Pippin in your part of the world."

A clerk came in with a typewritten sheet covered with Russian characters.

"Here's your letter of introduction to Kensky. He knows just as much English as you will want him to know."

When Malcolm presented himself at the lodgings, it was to discover that the old Jew had gone out, and had left no message as to the time he would return. Since Malcolm was anxious to meet this important personage, he did not leave his letter, but went into the City to lunch with an old college chum. In the afternoon he decided to make his call, and only remembered, as he was walking up the Strand, that he had intended satisfying his curiosity as to that "other neighbour" of his, the Grand Duke Yaroslav.

There was a little crowd about Charing Cross Station, though it was nearly two hours after midday when the Yaroslavs were due; and he was to discover, on inquiry of a policeman, that the cause of this public curiosity had been the arrival of two royal carriages.

"Some Russian prince or other," said the obliging bobby. "The boat was late, and—here they come!"

Malcolm was standing on the side-walk in the courtyard of Charing

Cross Station when the two open landaus drove out through the archway. In the first was a man a little over middle age, wearing a Russian uniform; but Malcolm had no eyes for him—it was for the girl who sat by his side, erect, haughty, almost disdainful, with her splendid beauty, and apparently oblivious to all that was being said to her by the smiling young man who sat on the opposite seat.

As the carriage came abreast and the postilions reined in their mounts before turning into the crowded Strand, the girl turned her head for a second and her eyes seemed to rest on Malcolm.

Instinctively he lifted his hat from his head, but it was not the girl who returned his salutation, but the stiff figure of the elderly man at her side who raised his hand with an automatic gesture. Only for a second, and then she swept out of view, and Malcolm heaved a long, deep sigh.

"Some dame!" said a voice at his side. "Well, I'm glad I saw him, anyway."

Malcolm looked down at the speaker. He was a stout little man, who wore his hard felt hat at a rakish angle. The butt of a fat cigar was clenched between his teeth, and his genial eyes met Malcolm's with an inviting frankness which was irresistible.

"That was his Grand Nibs, wasn't it?" asked the man, and Malcolm smiled.

"That was the Grand Duke, I think," he said.

"And who was the dame?"

"The dame?"

"I mean the lady, the young peacherino—gee! She was wonderful!"

Malcolm shared his enthusiasm but was not prepared to express himself with such vigour.

"That girl," said his companion, speaking with evident sincerity, "is wasted—what a face for a beauty chorus!"

Malcolm laughed. He was not a very approachable man, but there was something about this stranger which broke down all barriers.

"Well, I'm glad I've seen him," said Mr. Cherry Bim again emphatically. "I wonder what he's done."

Malcolm turned to move off, and the little man followed his example.

"What do you mean—what has he done?" asked the amused Malcolm.

"Oh, nothing," said the other airily, "but I just wondered, that's all."

"I'm glad I've seen them too," said Malcolm; "I nearly missed them. I was sitting so long over lunch——"

"You're a lucky man," said Mr. Bim.

"To have seen them?"

"No, to have sat over lunch," said Cherry with an inward groan. "My! I'd like to see what a lunch looks like."

Malcolm looked at the man with a new interest and a new sympathy.

"Broke?" he asked, and the other grinned.

"If I was only broke," he said, "there'd be no trouble. But what's the matter with me is that there ain't any pieces!"

Cherry Bim noticed the hesitation in Malcolm's face and said:

"I hope you're not worrying about hurting my feelings."

"How?" said the startled Malcolm.

"Why," drawled the other, "if it's among your mind that you'd like to slip me two dollars and you're afraid of me throwing it at you, why, you can get that out of your mind straightaway."

Malcolm laughed and handed half a sovereign to the man.

"Go and get something to eat," he said.

"Hold hard," said the other as Malcolm was turning away. "What is your name?"

"Does that matter?" asked the young man with amusement.

"It matters a lot to me," said the other seriously. "I like to pay back anything I borrow."

"Hay is my name—Malcolm Hay. It's no use giving you my address, because I shall be in Russia next week."

"In Russia, eh? That's rum!" Cherry Bim scratched his unshaven chin. "I'm always meeting Russians."

He looked at the young engineer thoughtfully, then, with a little jerk of his head and a "So long!" he turned and disappeared into the crowd.

Malcolm looked at his watch. He would try Kensky again, he thought; but again his mission was fruitless. He might have given up his search for this will-o'-the-wisp but for the fact that his new employers seemed to attach considerable importance to his making acquaintance with this notability of Kieff. He could hardly be out after dinner—he would try again.

He had dressed for the solitary meal, thinking that, if his quest again failed, he could spend the evening at a theatre. This time the elderly landlady of the house in which Mr. Kensky lodged informed him that her guest was at home; and a few moments later Malcolm was ushered into the presence of the old man.

Israel Kensky eyed his visitor keenly, taking him in from his carefully tied dress-bow to the tips of his polished boots. It was an approving glance, for Kensky, though he lived in one of the backwaters of civilization; though his attitude to the privileged classes of the world—in which category he placed Malcolm, did that young man but know it—was deferential and even servile; had very definite views as to what was, and was not, appropriate in his superior's attire.

He read through the letter which Malcolm had brought without a word, and then:

"Pray sit down, Mr. Hay," he said in English. "I have been expecting you. I had a letter from Mr. Tremayne."

Malcolm seated himself near the rough bench at which he cast curious eyes. The paraphernalia of Kensky's hobby still lay upon its surface.

"You are wondering what an old Jew does to amuse himself, eh?" chuckled Kensky. "Do you think we in South Russia do nothing but make bombs? If I had not an aptitude for business," he said (he pronounced the word "pizziness," and it was one of the few mispronunciations he made), "I should have been a bookbinder."

"It is beautiful work," said Malcolm, who knew something of the art.

"It takes my mind from things," said Kensky, "and also it helps me—yes, it helps me very much."

Malcolm did not ask him in what manner his craft might assist a millionaire merchant, for in those days he had not heard of the "Book of All-Power."

The conversation which followed travelled through awkward stages and more awkward pauses. Kensky looked a dozen times at the clock, and on the second occasion Malcolm, feeling uncomfortable, rose to go, but was eagerly invited to seat himself again.

"You are going to Russia?"

"Yes."

"It is a strange country if you do not know it. And the Russians are strange people. And to Kieff also! That is most important."

Malcolm did not inquire where the importance lay, and dismissed this as an oblique piece of politeness on the other's part.

"I am afraid I am detaining you, Mr. Kensky. I merely came in to make your acquaintance and shake hands with you," he said, rising, after yet another anxious glance at the clock on the part of his host.

"No, no, no," protested Kensky. "You must forgive me, Mr. Hay, if I seem to be dreaming and I do not entertain you. I am turning over in my mind so many possibilities, so many plans, and I think I have come to the right conclusion. You shall stay, and you shall know. I can rely upon your discretion, can I not?"

"Certainly, but——"

"I know I can!" said the old man, nodding "And you can help me. I am a stranger in London. Tell me, Mr. Hay, do you know the Café of the Silver Lion?"

The other was staggered by the question.

"No, I can't say that I do," he admitted. "I am a comparative stranger in London myself."

"Ah, but you can find it. You know all the reference books, which are so much Greek to me; you could discover it by inquiring of the police—inquiries made very discreetly, you understand, Mr. Hay?"

Malcolm wondered what he was driving at, but the old man changed the subject abruptly.

"To-night you will see a lady here. She is coming to me. Again I ask for your discretion and your silence. Wait!"

He shuffled to the window, pulled aside the blind and looked out.

"She is here," he said in a whisper. "You will stand just there."

He indicated a position which to Malcolm was ludicrously suggestive of his standing in a corner. Further explanations could neither be given nor asked for. The door opened suddenly and a girl came in, closing it behind her. She looked first at Kensky with a smile, and then at the stranger, and the smile faded from her lips. As for Malcolm, he was speechless. There was no doubt at all as to the identity. The straight nose, the glorious eyes, the full, parted lips.

Kensky shuffled across to her, bent down and kissed her hand.

"Highness," he said humbly, "this gentleman is a friend of mine. Trust old Israel Kensky, Highness!"

"I trust you, Israel Kensky," she replied in Russian, and with the sweetest smile that Malcolm had ever seen in a woman.

She bowed slightly to the young man, and for the rest of the interview her eyes and speech were for the Jew. He brought a chair forward for her, dusted it carefully, and she sat down by the table, leaning her chin on her palm, and looking at the old man.

"I could not come before," she said. "It was so difficult to get away."

"Your Highness received my letter?"

She nodded.

"But Israel," her voice almost pleaded, "you do not believe that this thing would happen?"

"Highness, all things are possible," said the old man. "Here in London the cellars and garrets teem with evil men."

"But the police——" she began.

"The police cannot shelter you, Highness, as they do in our Russia."

"I must warn the Grand Duke," she said thoughtfully, "and"—she hesitated, and a shadow passed over her face—"and the Prince. Is it not him they hate?"

Kensky shook his head.

"Lady," he said humbly, "in my letter I told you there was something which could not be put on paper, and that I will tell you now. And if I speak of very high matters, your Highness must forgive an old man."

She nodded, and again her laugh twinkled in her eyes.

"Your father, the Grand Duke Yaroslav," he said, "has one child, who is your Highness."

She nodded.

"The heir to the Grand Dukedom is——" He stopped inquiringly.

"The heir?" she said slowly. "Why, it is Prince Serganoff. He is with us."

Malcolm remembered the olive-faced young man who had sat on the seat of the royal carriage facing the girl; and instinctively he knew that this was Prince Serganoff, though in what relationship he stood to the Grand Ducal pair he had no means of knowing.

"The heir is Prince Serganoff," said the old man slowly, "and his Highness is an ambitious man. Many things can happen in our Russia, little lady. If the Grand Duke were killed——"

"Impossible!" She sprang to her feet. "He would never dare! He would never dare!"

Kensky spread out his expressive hands.

"Who knows?" he said. "Men and women are the slaves of their ambition."

She looked at him intently.

"He would never dare," she said slowly. "No, no, I cannot believe that."

The old man made no reply.

"Where did you learn this, Israel Kensky?" she asked.

"From a good source, Highness," he replied evasively, and she nodded.

"I know you would not tell me this unless there were some foundation," she said. "And your friend?" She looked inquiringly at the silent Hay. "Does he know?"

Israel Kensky shook his head.

"I would wish that the *gospodar* knew as much as possible, because he will be in Kieff, and who knows what will happen in Kieff? Besides, he knows London."

Malcolm did not attempt to deny the knowledge, partly because, in spite of his protest, he had a fairly useful working knowledge of the metropolis.

"I shall ask the *gospodar* to discover the meeting-place of the rabble."

"Do you suggest," she demanded, "that Prince Serganoff is behind this conspiracy, that he is the person who inspired this idea of assassination?"

Again the old man spread out his hands.

"The world is a very wicked place," he said.

"And the Prince has many enemies," she added with a bright smile. "You must know that, Israel Kensky. My cousin is Chief of the Political Police in St. Petersburg, and it is certain that people will speak against him."

The old man was eyeing her thoughtfully.

"Your Highness has much wisdom," he said, "and I remember, when you were a little girl, how you used to point out to me the bad men from the good. Tell me, lady, is Prince Serganoff a good man or a bad man? Is he capable or incapable of such a crime?"

She did not answer. In truth she could not answer; for all that Kensky had said, she had thought. She rose to her feet.

"I must go now, Israel Kensky," she said. "My car is waiting for me. I will write to you."

She would have gone alone, but Malcolm Hay, with amazing courage, stepped forward.

"If Your Imperial Highness will accept my escort to your car," he said humbly, "I shall be honoured."

She looked at him in doubt.

"I think I would rather go alone."

"Let the young man go with you, Highness," said Kensky earnestly. "I shall feel safer in my mind."

She nodded, and led the way down the stairs. They turned out of the garden into the street and did not speak a word. Presently the girl said in English:

"You must think we Russian people are barbarians, Mr.——"

"Hay," suggested Malcolm.

"Mr. Hay. That is Scottish, isn't it? Tell me, do you think we are uncivilized?"

"No, Your Highness," stammered Malcolm. "How can I think that?"

They walked on until they came in sight of the tail lights of the car, and then she stopped.

"You must not come any farther," she said. "You can stand here and watch me go. Do you know any more than Israel Kensky told?" she asked, a little anxiously.

"Nothing," he replied in truth.

She offered her hand, and he bent over it.

"Good night, Mr. Hay. Do not forget, I must see you in Kieff."

He watched the red lights of the car disappear and walked quickly back to old Kensky's rooms. Russia and his appointment had a new fascination.

Chapter 4

THE PRINCE WHO PLANNED

Few people knew or know how powerful a man Prince Serganoff really was in these bad old days. He waved his hand and thousands of men and women disappeared. He beckoned and he had a thousand sycophantic suppliants.

In the days before he became Chief of the Police to the entourage, he went upon a diplomatic mission to High Macedonia, the dark and sinister state. He was sent by none, but he had a reason, for Dimitrius, his sometime friend, had fled to the capital of the higher Balkan state and Serganoff went down without authority to terrify his sometime confidant into returning for trial. In High Macedonia the exquisite young man was led by sheer curiosity to make certain inquiries into the domestic administration of the country, and learnt things.

He had hardly made himself master of these before he was sent for by the Foreign Minister.

"Highness," said the suave man, stroking his long, brown beard, "how long have you been in the capital?"

"Some four days, Excellency," said the Prince.

"That is ninety-six hours too long," said the minister. "There is a train for the north in forty minutes. You will catch that, and God be with you!"

Prince Serganoff did not argue but went out from the ornate office, and the Minister called a man who was waiting.

"If his Highness does not leave by the four o'clock train, cut his throat and carry the body to one of the common houses of the town—preferably that of the man Domopolo, the Greek, who is a bad character, and well deserving of death."

"Excellency," said the man gravely, and saluted his way out.

They knew Serganoff in High Macedonia and were a little anxious. Had they known him better they would have feared him less. He did not leave by the four o'clock train, but by a special which was across the frontier by four. He sat in a cold sweat till the frontier post was past.

This man was a mass of contradictions. He liked the good things of life. He bought his hosiery in Paris, his shoes in Vienna, his suits and cravats in New York; and it is said of him that he made a special pilgrimage to London—the Mecca of those who love good leather work—for the characteristic attaché cases which were so indispensable to the Chief of Gendarmerie of the Marsh Town.

He carried with him the irrepressible trimness and buoyancy of youth, with his smooth, sallow face, his neat black moustache and his shapeliness of outline. An exquisite of exquisites, he had never felt the draughts of life or experienced its rude buffetings.

His perfectly-appointed flat in the Morskaya had been modelled to his taste and fancy. It was a suite wherein you pressed buttons and comfortable things happened. You opened windows and boiled water, or summoned a valet to your bedside by the gentle pressure you applied to a mother-of-pearl stud set in silver plate which, by some miracle, was always within reach.

He had an entire suite converted to bath-rooms, where his masseur, his manicurist and his barber attended him daily. He had conscripted modern science to his service, he had so cunningly disguised its application, that you might never guess the motive power of the old English clock which ticked in the spacious hall, or realize that the soft light which came from the many branched candelabra which hung from the centre of his drawing-room was due to anything more up to date than the hundred most life-like candles which filled the sockets.

Yet this suave gentleman with his elegant manners and his pretty taste in old china, this genius who was the finest judge in the capital of Pekinese dogs, and had been known to give a thousand-rouble fee to the veterinary surgeon who performed a minor operation on his favourite Borzoi, had another aspect. He who shivered at the first chill winds of winter and wrapped himself in sables whenever he drove abroad after the last days of September, and had sent men and women to the bleakness of Alexandrowski without a qualm; he who had to fortify himself to face an American dentist (his fees for missed appointments would have kept the average middle-class family in comfort for a year), was ruthless in his dealings with the half-crazed men and women who strayed across the frontier which divided conviction from propaganda.

Physical human suffering left him unmoved—he hanged the murderer Palatoff with his own hands. Yet in that operation someone saw him turn very pale and shrink back from his victim. Afterwards the reason was discovered. The condemned man had had the front of his rough shirt fastened with a safety-pin which had worked loose. The point had ripped a little gash in the inexperienced finger of the amateur hangman.

He brought Dr. Von Krauss from Berlin, because von Krauss was an authority upon blood infection and spent a week of intense mental agony until he was pronounced out of danger.

He sat before a long mirror in his bedroom, that gave on Horridge's Hotel, and surveyed himself thoughtfully. He was looking at the only man he trusted, for it was not vanity, but a love of agreeable company that explained the passion for mirrors which was the jest of St. Petersburg.

It was his fourth day in London and a little table near the window was covered with patterns of cloth; he had spent an exciting afternoon with the representative of his tailor. But it was not of sartorial magnificence that he was thinking.

He stretched out his legs comfortably towards his reflection, and smiled.

"Yes," he said, as though answering some secret thought, and he and the reflection nodded to one another as though they had reached a complete understanding.

Presently he pushed the bell and his valet appeared.

"Has the Grand Duke gone?" he asked.

"Yes, Excellency," replied the man.

"And the Grand Duchess?"

"Yes, Excellency."

"Good!" Serganoff nodded.

"Is your Excellency's headache better?" asked the man.

"Much better," replied the Chief of Police. "Go to their Highness's suite, and tell their servant—what is the man's name?"

"Boolba, Excellency," said the valet.

"Yes, that is the fellow. Ask him to come to me. The Grand Duke mentioned a matter which I forgot to tell Boolba."

Boolba made his appearance, a suave domestic, wearing the inconspicuous livery of an English butler rather than the ornate uniform which accompanied his office in Kieff.

"That will do." Serganoff dismissed his valet. "Boolba, come here."

The man approached him and Serganoff lowered his voice.

"You have made a fool of me again, Boolba."

"Excellency," pleaded the man urgently, "I have done all that was possible."

"You have placed my fortune and my life in the hands of an American criminal. If that is your idea of doing all that is possible, I agree with you," said Serganoff. "Be careful, Boolba! The arm of the Bureau is a very long one, and greater men than you have disappeared from their homes."

"Illustrious Excellency," said the agitated man, "I swear to you I did all that you requested. There were many reasons why I should not entrust this matter to the men of the secret society."

"I should like to hear a few," said Serganoff, cleaning his nails delicately.

"Excellency, the Grand Duke stands well with the society. He had never oppressed them, and he is the only popular member of the Imperial House with our—their society."

"Our society, eh?" said Serganoff, noticing the slip. "Go on."

"Besides, Excellency," said Boolba, "it was necessary not only to kill the Grand Duke, but to shoot down his assassin. Our plan was to get this American to shoot him in the park, where he walks in the morning, and then for one of the society to shoot the American. That was a good plan, because it meant that the man who could talk would talk no more, and that the comrade who shot down the murderer would stand well with the Government."

Serganoff nodded.

"And your plan has failed," he said, "failed miserably at the outset. You dog!"

He leapt to his feet, his eyes blazing, and Boolba stepped back.

"Highness, wait, wait!" he cried. "I have something else in my mind! I could have helped Highness better if I had known more. But I could only guess. I had to grope in the dark all the time."

"Do you imagine I am going to take you into my confidence?" asked Serganoff. "What manner of fool am I? Tell me what you have guessed. You may sit down; nobody will come in, and if they do you can be buttoning my boots."

Boolba wiped his damp face with a handkerchief and leaned nearer to the man.

"If the Grand Duke dies, a certain illustrious person succeeds to his estates," he said, "but not to his title."

Serganoff looked at him sharply. The man had put into words the one difficulty which had occupied the mind of the Chief of Police for months.

"Well?" he said.

"The title is in the gift of the Czar," said Boolba. "He alone can create a Grand Duke who succeeds but is not in the direct line. Therefore, the killing of Yaroslav would bring little but the property to the illustrious person. Only if His Imperial Majesty decided upon a worthier holder, or if the Grand Duke fell under a cloud at Court, could it pass to the illustrious person."

"That I know," said Serganoff. "Well?"

"Well, Highness, would it not be better if the Grand Duke were disgraced, if he were brought to St. Petersburg to answer certain charges which the illustrious person formulated? After, the Grand Duke might die—that is a simple matter. Russia would think that he had been put to death by the Court party as a matter of policy. Yaroslav is not in favour at the Court," he added significantly; but Serganoff shook his head.

"He is not sufficiently out of favour yet," he said. "Go on, man, you have something in your mind."

Boolba edged closer.

"Suppose the Grand Duke or the Grand Duchess were involved in some conspiracy against the Imperial House?" he said, speaking rapidly. "Suppose, on evidence which could not be disputed, such as the evidence of the London police, it was proved that either the Grand Duke or his daughter was in league with an anarchist society, or was attending their meetings—does your Excellency see?"

"I see," said Serganoff, "but they do not attend meetings."

Boolba hesitated.

"Yet," he said, speaking slowly, "I would guarantee that I could bring the Grand Duchess Irene to such a meeting, and that I could arrange for the place to be raided whilst she was there."

Serganoff put down his orange stick and eyed the other keenly.

"You have brains, Boolba," he said. "Some day I shall bring you to St. Petersburg and place you on my staff—if you do not know too much."

He paced the apartment, his hands clasped behind his back.

"Suppose you get in touch with this American again, bring him to the meeting, unless he's afraid to come, and then boldly suggest to him that he goes to St. Petersburg to make an attempt upon the life of the Czar himself."

"He would reject it," said Boolba, shaking his head.

"What if he did—that doesn't matter," said Serganoff impatiently. "It is sufficient that the suggestion is made. Suppose this man is amongst these infamous fellows when the London police raid and arrest them, and he makes a statement that he was approached to destroy the Imperial life, and the Grand Duchess Irene is arrested at the same time?"

Boolba's eyes brightened.

"That is a wonderful idea, Highness," he said admiringly.

Serganoff continued his pacing, and presently stopped.

"I will arrange the police raid," he said. "I am in communication with Scotland Yard, and it will be better if I am present when the raid is conducted. It is necessary that I should identify myself with this chapter," he said, "but how will you induce the Grand Duchess to come?"

"Leave that to me, Highness," replied the man, and gave some details of his scheme.

Chapter 5

THE RAID ON THE SILVER LION

Sophia Kensky was a loyal and faithful adherent to the cause she had espoused, and her report, written in the weird caligraphy of Russia, greatly interested the butler of the Grand Duke Yaroslav. From that report he learned of the visit which the Grand Duchess Irene had paid; learned, too, that she had been escorted to her car by an Englishman, whose name the woman did not know; and was to discover later that the said "Englishman" had been sent out by Israel Kensky on a special mission. That mission was to discover the Silver Lion, a no very difficult task. In point of fact, it was discoverable in a London telephone directory, because the upper part of the premises were used legitimately enough in the proprietor's business as restaurateur.

Malcolm Hay had lunch at the place and saw nothing suspicious in its character. Most of the clientèle were obviously foreign, and not a few were Russian. Pretending to lose his way, he wandered through the service door, and there made the important discovery that the kitchen was on the top floor, and also that meals were being served somewhere in the basement. This he saw during the few minutes he was allowed to make observations, because there was a service lift which was sent down to the unseen clients below.

He apologized for his intrusion and went out. Officially there was no basement-room, nor, from the restaurant itself, any sign of stairs which led down to an underground chamber. He made a further reconnaissance, and found the back door which Sophia Kensky had described in her hypnotic sleep, and the location of which the old man had endeavoured to convey to his agent.

Malcolm Hay was gifted with many of the qualities which make up the equipment of a good detective. In addition, he had the education and training of an engineer. That the underground room existed, he knew by certain structural evidence, and waited about in the street until he saw three men come out and the door close behind them. After awhile, another two emerged. There was nothing sinister or romantic about the existence of a basement dining-room, or even of a basement club-room.

The character of this club was probably well known to the police, he thought, and pursued his inquiries to Marlborough Street police station. There he found, as he had expected, that the club was registered and known as "The Foreign Friends of Freedom Club." The officer who supplied him with the information told him that the premises were visited at frequent intervals by a representative of the police, and that nothing of an irregular character had been reported.

"Have you any complaints to make?" asked the official.

"None whatever," smiled Hay. "Only I am writing an article on the foreign clubs of London, and I want to be sure of my facts."

It was the first and most plausible lie that occurred to him, and it answered his purpose. He returned to Kensky with his information, and the old man producing a map of London, he marked the spot with a red cross. All this time Malcolm Hay was busy making preparations for departure. He would have been glad to stay on, so that his leaving London would coincide with the departure of the Grand Duchess, but his sleeper had already been booked, and he had to make a call *en route* at Vienna.

It was on the occasion of this visit with details of the location and character of the club, that he first saw Sophia Kensky. He thought her pretty in a bold, heavy way, and she regarded him with insolent indifference. It was one of the few occasions in his life that he spoke with her.

"The *gospodar* is going to Kieff, Sophia Kensky," introduced the old man.

"What will you do in Kieff, Excellency?" asked the woman indolently.

"I shall not be in Kieff," smiled Hay, "except on rare occasions. I am taking charge of some oil-wells about twenty versts outside of the town."

"It is a terrible life, living in the country," she said, and he was inclined to agree.

This and a few trite sentiments about Russian weather and Russian seasons were the only words he ever exchanged with her in his life. Years later, when he stood, hardly daring to breathe, in the cupboard of a commissary's office, and heard her wild denunciation of the man who had sent her to death, he was to recall this first and only meeting.

Israel Kensky dismissed his daughter without ceremony, and it was then that Malcolm Hay told him the result of his investigations. The old man sat for a long time stroking his beard.

"Two more days they stay in this town," he said, half to himself, "and that is the dangerous time."

He looked up sharply at Hay.

"You are clever, and you are English," he said. "Would you not help an old man to save this young life from misery and sorrow?"

Malcolm Hay looked at him in astonishment.

"To save whom?" he asked.

"The Grand Duchess," replied Kensky moodily. "It is for her I fear, more than for her father."

Malcolm Hay was on the point of blurting out the very vital truth that there was nothing in the wide world he would not do to save that wonderful being from the slightest ache or pain, but thought it best to dissemble the craziest of infatuations that ever a penniless and obscure engineer felt for a daughter of the Imperial House of Russia. Instead he murmured some conventional expression of his willingness.

"It is in this club that the danger lies," said Kensky. "I know these societies, Mr. Hay, and I fear them most when they look most innocent."

"Could you not get the police to watch?" asked Malcolm.

Had he lived in Russia, or had he had the experience which was his in the following twelve months, he would not have asked so absurd a question.

"No, no," said Kensky, "this is not a matter for the police. It is a matter for those who love her."

"What can I do?" asked Malcolm hastily.

He had a horrible feeling that his secret had been surprised, for he was of the age when love is fearless of everything except ridicule.

"You could watch the club," said Kensky. "I myself would go, but I am too old, and this English weather makes me sick."

"You mean actually watch it?" said Malcolm in surprise. "Why, I'll do that like a shot!"

"Note who goes in and who come out," said Kensky. "Be on hand at all times, in case you are called upon for help. You will see my daughter there," he said, after a pause, and a faint smile curved his pale lips. "Yes, Sophia Kensky is a great conspirator!"

"Whom do you expect me to see?" asked the other bluntly.

Kensky got up from his chair and went to a leather bag which stood on the sideboard. This he unlocked, and from a mass of papers took a photograph. He brought it back to the young man.

"Why," said Malcolm in surprise, "that is the man Serganoff, the Prince fellow!"

Kensky nodded slowly.

"That is Serganoff," he said. "Here is another picture of him, but not of his face."

It was, in fact, a snapshot photograph showing the back of the Police Chief; and it might have been, thought Malcolm, of a tailor's dummy, with its wasp waist and its perfectly creased trousers.

"Particularly I wish to know whether he will visit the club in the next two days," said the old man. "It is important that you should look for him."

"Anybody else?"

Kensky hesitated.

"I hope not," he said. "I hope not!"

Malcolm Hay went back to his hotel, feeling a new zest in life. His experience of the past few days had been incredible. He, an unknown student, had found himself suddenly plunged into the heart of an anarchist plot, and on nodding terms with royal highnesses! He laughed softly as he sat on the edge of his bed and reviewed all the circumstances, but did not laugh when the thought occurred to him that the danger which might be threatening this girl was very real.

That side of the adventure sobered him. He had sense enough to see that it was the unalienable right of youth to believe in fairies and to love beautiful princesses, and that such passions were entitled to disturb the rest and obscure the judgment of their victims for days and even for weeks. But he had an unpleasant conviction that he was looking at the Grand Duchess from an angle which was outside his experience of fairy stories.

That night when he went on his way to take up his "police duty" in the little street behind the Silver Lion, he saw two mounted policemen trotting briskly down the Strand followed by a closed carriage, and in the light of the electric standard he caught a glimpse of a face which set his heart beating faster. He cursed himself for his folly, swore so vigorously and so violently at his own stupidity, that he did not realize he was talking aloud, until the open-mouthed indignation of an elderly lady brought him to a sense of decorum.

She was going to the theatre, of course, he thought, and wondered what theatre would be graced by her presence. He half regretted his promise to Israel Kensky, which prevented him discovering the house of entertainment and securing a box or a stall from whence he could feast his eyes upon her face.

His vigil was painfully monotonous. It was the most uninteresting job he had ever undertaken. Most of the habitués of the club had evidently come at an early hour, for he saw nobody come in and nobody go out until nearly eleven o'clock. It began to rain a fine, thin drizzle, which penetrated every crevice, which insinuated itself down his neck, though his collar was upturned; and then, on top of this, came a gusty easterly wind, which chilled him to the marrow. Keeping in the shadow of the houses opposite, he maintained, however, a careful scrutiny, thereby earning the suspicion of a policeman, who passed him twice on his beat before he stopped to ask if he were looking for somebody.

As midnight chimed from a neighbouring church the door of the club opened and its members came out. Malcolm crossed the road and walked down to meet them, since they all seemed to be coming in the same direction.

There were about twenty men, and they were speaking in Russian or Yiddish, but the subjects of their discourse were of the most innocent character. He saw nobody he knew, or had ever seen before. Israel Kensky had expected that the St. Petersburg Chief of Police would be present; that expectation was not realized. Then he heard the door bolted and chained, and went home, after the most unprofitable evening he had ever spent.

How much better it would have been to sit in the warm theatre, with, perhaps, a clear view of the girl, watching her every movement, seeing her smile, noting her little tricks of manner or gesture.

In the end he laughed himself into a sane condition of mind, ate a hearty supper, and went to bed to dream that Serganoff was pursuing him with a hammer in his hand, and that the Grand Duchess was sitting in a box wildly applauding the efforts of her homicidal relative.

The next afternoon Malcolm Hay was packing, with the remainder of his belongings, a few articles he had purchased in London. Amongst these was a small and serviceable Colt revolver, and he stood balancing this in the palm of his hand, uncertain as to whether it would not be better to retain his weapon until after his present adventure. Twice he put it into his portmanteau and twice took it out again, and finally, blushing at the act, he slipped the weapon into his hip-pocket.

He felt theatrical and cheap in doing so. He told himself that he was investing a very common-place measure of precaution taken by old Israel Kensky, who was probably in the secret police, to protect his protégée, with an importance and a romance which it did not deserve. He went down to his post that night, feeling horribly self-conscious.

This time he kept on the same side of the street as that on which the club was situated.

His watch was rewarded by events of greater interest than had occurred on the previous night. He had not been on duty half an hour before two men walked rapidly from the end of the street and passed him so closely that he could not make any mistake as to the identity of one. Had he not been able to recognize him, his voice would have instantly betrayed his identity, for, as they passed, the shorter of the two was talking.

"I'm one of those guys who don't believe in starving to death in a delicatessen store——"

Malcolm looked after the pair in amazement. It was the little man whom he had befriended in the courtyard at Charing Cross station. Other people drifted through the door in ones and twos, and then a man came walking smartly across the street, betraying the soldier at every stride. Malcolm turned and strolled in his direction.

There was no mistaking him either, though he was muffled up to the chin. With his tight-waisted greatcoat, a glimpse of an olive face with two piercing dark eyes, which flashed an inquiring glance as they passed—there was no excuse for error. It was Colonel Prince Serganoff beyond a doubt.

A quarter of an hour later came the real shock of the evening. A girl was almost on top of him before he saw her, for she was wearing shoes which made no sound. He had only time to turn so that she did not see his face, before she too entered the door and passed in. The Grand Duchess! And Serganoff! And the American adventurer!

What had these three in common, he wondered. And now he recalled the warning of the old man. Perhaps the girl was in danger— the thought brought him to the door, with his hand raised and touching the bell-push before he realized his folly. There was nothing to do but wait.

Five minutes passed and ten minutes, and then Malcolm Hay became conscious of the fact that something unusual was happening in the street. It was more thickly populated. Half a dozen men had appeared at either end of the street and were moving slowly towards him, as though——

And then in a flash he realized just what was happening. It was a police raid. In his student days he had seen such a raid upon a gambling house, and he recognized all the signs. He first thought of the girl—she must not be involved in this. He raced toward the door, but somebody had ran quicker, and his hand was on the bell-push when he was swung violently backwards, and an authoritative voice said:

"Take that man, sergeant."

A hand gripped his shoulder and somebody peered in his face.

"Why, he's English," he said in surprise.

"Yes, yes," gasped Malcolm. "I'm sorry to interfere, but there is a lady in there, in whom I'm rather interested—you're raiding this club, aren't you?"

"That's about the size of it," said a man in civilian clothes; and then, suspiciously, "Who are you?"

Malcolm explained his status and calling.

"Take my advice and get away. Don't be mixed up in this business," said the officer. "You can release him, sergeant. What's the time?"

A clock struck at that moment, and the officer in charge of the raid pressed the bell.

"If you've a lady friend involved in this, perhaps you'd like to stand by," he said. "She may want you to bail her out," he added good-humouredly.

Chapter 6

Prince Serganoff Pays the Price

Mr. Cherry Bim, a citizen of the world, and an adventurer at large, was an optimist to his finger-tips. He also held certain races in profound contempt, not because he knew the countries, but because he had met representatives of those nations in America, and judged by their characteristics.

So that the man called Yakoff, whose task it was to inveigle Mr. Bim again to the premises of the Friends of Freedom Club, found to his astonishment that Mr. Bim required very little inveigling. The truth was, of course, that the gun-man had a supreme contempt for all Russians, whom he had classified mistakenly as "Lithanians" and "Pollaks." To the fervent promise made by Mr. Yakoff that no harm would come to him, Cherry Bim had replied briefly but unprintably.

"Of course, there'll be no harm come to me," he said scornfully. "You don't think I worry about what that bunch will do? No, sir! But I'm powerfully disinclined to associate myself with people out of my class. It doesn't do a man any good to be seen round with Pollaks and Letts."

Yakoff earnestly implored him to come and give the benefit of his experience to the assembly, and had promised him substantial payment. This latter argument was one which Cherry Bim could understand and appreciate. He accepted on the spot, and came down to the stuffy little underground room, expecting no more than to be asked to deliver a lecture on the gentle art of assassination. Not that he knew very much about it, because Cherry, with three or four men to his credit, had shot them in fair fight; but a hundred pounds was a lot of money, and he badly needed just enough to shake the mud of England from his shoes and seek a land more prolific in possibilities.

The first thing he noticed on arrival was that Boolba, the man who had interrogated him before, was not present. In his place sat a smaller man, with a straggly black beard and a white face, who was addressed as "Nicholas."

The second curious circumstance which struck him was that he was received also in an ominous silence.

The black-bearded man, who spoke in perfect English, indicated a chair to the left of him.

"Sit down, comrade," he said. "We have asked you to come because we have another proposition to make to you."

"If it's a croaking proposition, you needn't go any farther," said Cherry, "and I won't trouble you with my presence, gents, and——" he looked in vain for the woman he had seen before, and added, that he might round off his sentence gracefully—"fellow murderers."

"Mr. Bim," said Nicholas in his curious singsong tone, "does it not make your blood boil to see tyranny in high places——"

"Now, can that stuff!" said Cherry Bim. "Nothing makes my blood boil, or would make my blood boil, except sitting on a stove, I guess. Tyranny don't mean any more in my young life than Hennessy, and tyrants more than hydrants. I guess I was brought up in a land of freedom and glory, where the only tyrant you ever meet is a traffic cop. If this is another croaking job, why, gents, I won't trouble you any longer."

He half-rose, but Nicholas pushed him down.

"Not even if it was the Czar?" he said calmly.

Cherry Bim gaped at him.

"The Czar?" he said, with a queer little grimace to emphasize his disbelief in the evidence of his hearing. "What are you getting at?"

"Would you shoot the Czar for two thousand pounds?" asked Nicholas.

Cherry Bim pushed his hat to the back of his head and got up, shaking off the protesting arm.

"I'm through," he said, "and that's all there is to it."

It was at that moment that Serganoff came through the door and Cherry Bim remained where he stood, surprised to silence, for the face of the newcomer was covered from chin to forehead by a black silk mask.

The door was shut behind him; he walked slowly to the table and dropped into a broken chair, Cherry's eyes never leaving his face.

"For fifteen years," said the gun-man, speaking slowly, "I've been a crook, but never once have I seen a guy got up like that villain in a movie picture. Say, mister, let's have a look at your face."

Cherry Bim was not the only person perturbed by the arrival of a masked stranger. Only three men in the room were in the secret of the newcomer's identity, and suspicious and scowling faces were turned upon him.

"You will excuse me," said the mask, "but there are many reasons why you should not see me or know me again."

"And there's a mighty lot of reasons why you shouldn't know me again," said Cherry, "yet I've obliged you with a close-up of my distinguished features."

"You have heard the proposition," said the man. "What do you think of it?"

"I think it's a fool proposition," replied Cherry contemptuously. "I've told these lads before that I am not falling for the Lucretia Borgia stuff, and I'm telling you the same."

The masked man chuckled.

"Well, don't let us quarrel," he said. "Nicholas, give him the money we promised."

Nicholas put his hand in his pocket and brought out a roll of notes, which he tossed to the man on his left, and Cherry Bim, to whom tainted money was as acceptable as tainted pheasant to the epicure, pocketed it with a smack of his lips.

"Now, if there's anything I can do for you boys," he said, "here's your chance to make use of me. Though I say it myself, there ain't a man in New York with my experience, tact and finesse. Show me a job that can be done single-handed, with a dividend at the end of it, and I'll show you a man who can take it on. In the meantime," said he affably, "the drinks are on me. Call the waiter, and order the best in the house."

Serganoff held up his hand.

"Wait," he said; "was that the door?"

Nicholas nodded, and the whole room stood in silence and watched the door slowly open. There was a gasp of astonishment, of genuine surprise, for Irene Yaroslav was well known to them, and it was Irene Yaroslav who stood with her back to the door. She wore a long black cloak of sable and by her coiffure it was evident that she was wearing an evening toilette beneath the cloak.

"Where is Israel Kensky?" she asked.

She did not immediately see the man in the masked face, for he sat under a light and his broad-brimmed hat threw his face into shadow.

Nobody answered her, and she asked again:

"Where is Israel Kensky?"

"He is not here," said Serganoff coolly, as she took two paces and stopped dead, clasping her hands before her.

"What does this mean?" she asked. "What are you doing here, Ser——"

"Stop!" His voice was almost a shout, and yet there was a shake in it.

Serganoff realized the danger of his own position, if amongst these men were some who had cause to hate him.

"Do not mention my name, Irene."

"What are you doing here?" she asked. "And where is Israel Kensky?"

"He has not come," Serganoff's voice was uneven and his hands shook.

She turned to go, but he was before her and stood with his back to the entrance.

"You will wait," he said.

"What insolence is this?" she demanded haughtily. "I had a letter from Israel Kensky telling me to come here under his protection and I should learn the truth of the plot against my father."

Serganoff had recovered something of his self-possession and laughed softly.

"It was I who sent you that letter, Irene. I sent it because I particularly desired you here at this moment."

"You shall pay for this," she said, and tried to force her way past him, but his strong hands gripped her and pushed her back.

She turned with a flaming face upon the men.

"Are you men," she asked, "that you allow this villain, who betrayed my father and will betray you, to treat a woman so."

She spoke in Russian, and nobody moved. Then a voice said:

"Speak English, miss."

She turned and glanced gratefully at the stout little man with his grotesque Derby hat and his good-humoured smile.

"I have been brought here by a trick," she said breathlessly, "by this man"—she pointed to Serganoff. "Will you help me leave? You're English, aren't you?"

"American, miss," said Cherry Bim. "And as for helping you, why, bless you, you can class me as your own little bodyguard."

"Stop!" cried Serganoff hoarsely, and instinctively, at the sight of the levelled revolver. Cherry's hands went up. "You'll keep out of this and do not interfere," said Serganoff. "You'll have all the trouble you want before this evening is through. Irene, come here."

At one side of the room was a narrow doorway, which most of the members believed led to a cupboard, but which a few knew was a safety bolt in case of trouble. The Prince had recognized the door by its description, and had edged his way towards it, taking the key from his pocket.

He gripped the girl by the waist, inserted the key and flung open the door. She struggled to escape, but the hand that held the key also held the revolver, and never once did it point anywhere but at Cherry Bim's anatomy.

"Help!" cried the girl. "This man is Serganoff, the Chief of Police at Petrograd——"

There was a crash, and the sound of hurrying footsteps. A voice from the outer hall screamed, "The police!"

At that moment Serganoff dragged the girl through the doorway and slammed it behind him. They were in a small cellar, almost entirely filled with barrels, with only a narrow alley-way left to reach a farther door. He dragged her through this apartment, up a short flight of stairs. They were on the level of the restaurant, and the girl could hear the clatter of plates as he pushed her up another stairway and into a room. By its furniture she guessed it was a private dining-room. The blinds were drawn and she had no means of knowing whether the apartment overlooked the front or the back of the premises.

He stopped long enough to lock the door and then he turned to her, slipping off his mask.

"I thought you would recognize me," he said coolly.

"What does this outrage mean?" asked the girl with heaving bosom. "You shall pay for this, colonel."

"There will be a lot of payment to be made before this matter is through," he said calmly. "Calm yourself, Irene. I have saved you from a great disgrace. Are you aware that, at the moment I brought you from that room, the English police were raiding it?"

"I should not have been in the room but for you," she said, "my father——"

"It is about your father I want to speak," he said. "Irene, I am the sole heir to your father's estate. Beyond the property which is settled on you, you have nothing. My affection for you is known and approved at Court."

"Your affection!" she laughed bitterly. "I'd as soon have the affection of a wolf!"

"You could not have a more complete wolf than I," he said meaningly. "Do you know what has happened to-night? An anarchist club in London has been raided, and the Grand Duchess Irene Yaroslav has been found in the company of men whose object is to destroy the monarchy."

She realized with a sickening sense of disaster all that it meant. She knew as well as he in what bad odour her father stood at Court, and guessed the steps which would be taken if this matter became public.

"I was brought here by a trick," she said steadily. "A letter came to me, as I thought, from Israel Kensky——"

"It was from me," he interrupted.

"And you planned the raid, of course?"

He nodded.

"I planned the raid in the most promising circumstances," he said. "The gentleman who offered to be your good knight is a well-known New York gun-man. He is wanted by the police, who probably have him in their custody at this moment. He was brought here to-night, and an offer was made to him, an offer of a large sum of money, on condition that he would destroy the Czar."

She gasped.

"You see, my little Irene, that when this gun-man's evidence is taken in court, matters will look very bad for the Yaroslav family."

"What do you propose?" she asked.

"There are two alternatives," he said. "The first is that I should arrest you and hand you over to the police. The second is that you should undertake most solemnly to marry me, in which case I will take you away from here."

She was silent.

"Is there a third possibility?" she asked, and he shook his head.

"My dear," he said familiarly as he flicked a speck of dust from his sleeve. "I think you will take the easier way. None of these scum will betray you, thinking that you are one of themselves—as I happen to know, some of the best families in Russia are associated with plotters of this type. As for the American, who might be inclined to talk, in a few weeks he will be on his way to New York to serve a life sentence. I have been looking up his record, and particularly drew the attention of the English police to the fact that he would be here to-night."

Cherry Bim, creeping up the stairs in his stockinged feet—he had marked and shot the fuse-box to pieces before the police came in, and had burst his way through the door in the wall—heard the sound of voices in the little room and stopped to listen. It was not a thick door, and he could hear Serganoff's voice very clearly. He stooped down to the key-hole. Serganoff had not taken the key out, and it was an old-fashioned key, the end of which projected an eighth of an inch on the other side of the door. Cherry Bim felt in his pocket and produced a pair of peculiarly shaped nippers, and gripped the end of the key, turning it gently. Then he slipped his handy gun from his pocket and waited.

"Now, Irene," said Serganoff's voice. "You must decide. In a few minutes the police will be up here, for they are instructed to make a complete search of the house. I can either explain that you are here to witness the raid, or that I have followed you up and arrested you. Which is it to be?"

Still she did not answer. Serganoff had laid his revolver on the table and this she was manoeuvring to reach. He divined her intention before she sprang forward, and, gripping her by the waist, threw her back.

"That will be more useful to me than to you," he said.

"Sure thing it will!" said a voice behind him.

He turned as swift as a cat and fired. The horrified girl heard only one shot, so quickly did one report follow another. She saw Cherry Bim raise his hand and wipe the blood from his cheek, saw the splinter of wood where the bullet had struck behind him; then Serganoff groaned and sprawled forward over the table. She dared not look at him, but followed Bim's beckoning finger.

"Down the stairs and out of that door, miss," he said, "or the bulls will have you."

She did not ask him who the "bulls" were; she could guess. She flew down the stairs, with trembling hands unfastened the lock and stepped into the street. It was empty, save for two men, and one of these came forward to meet her with outstretched hands.

"Thank God you're safe!" he said. "You weren't there, were you?"

Malcolm Hay was incoherent. The detective who was with him could but smile a little, for the girl had come out of the door which, according to his instructions, led only to the private dining-room.

"Take me away," she whispered.

He put his arm about her trembling figure, and led her along the street. All the time he was in terror lest the police should call her back, and desire him to identify her; but nothing happened and they gained Shaftesbury Avenue and a blessed taxicab.

"To Israel Kensky," she said. "I can't go home like this."

He stretched out of the window and gave fresh instructions.

"I am greatly obliged to you, Mr. Hay," she faltered and then covered her face with her hands. "Oh, it was dreadful, dreadful!"

"What happened?" he asked.

She shook her head. Then suddenly:

"No, no, I must go home. Will you tell the cabman? There is a chance that I may get into my suite without Boolba seeing. Will you go on to Israel Kensky after you have left me, and tell him what has happened?"

He nodded, and again gave the change of instructions.

They reached the hotel at a period when most of the guests were either lingering over their dinner or had gone to the theatre.

"I hate leaving you like this," he said; "how do I know that you will get in without detection?"

She smiled in spite of her distress.

"You're an inventor, aren't you, Mr. Hay?" she laughed. "But I am afraid even you could not invent a story which would convince my father if he knew I had been to that horrible place." Presently she said: "My room overlooks the street. If I get in without detection I will come to the window and wave a handkerchief."

He waited in a fit of apprehension, until presently he saw a light leap up to three windows, and her figure appeared. There was a flutter of a white handkerchief, and the blinds were drawn. Malcolm Hay drove to Maida Vale, feeling that the age of romance was not wholly dead.

To his surprise Kensky had had the news before he reached there.

"Is she safe? Is she safe?" asked the old man tremulously. "Now, thank Jehovah for his manifold blessings and mercies! I feared something was wrong. Her Highness wrote to me this afternoon, and I did not get the letter," said Israel. "They waylaid the messenger, and wrote and told her to go to the Silver Lion—the devils!"

His hand was shaking as he took up the poker to stir the fire.

"He, at any rate, will trouble none of us again," he said with malignant satisfaction.

"He? Who?"

"Serganoff," said the old man. "He was dead when the police found him!"

"And the American?" asked Hay.

"Only Russians were arrested," said Israel Kensky. "I do not think I shall see him again."

In this he was wrong, though six years were to pass before they met: the mystic, Israel Kensky, Cherry Bim the modern knight-errant, and Malcolm Hay.

Chapter 7

KENSKY OF KIEFF

Malcolm Hay drew rein half a verst from the Church of St. Andrea. Though his shaggy little horse showed no signs of distress, Malcolm kicked his feet free from the stirrups and descended, for his journey had been a long one, the day was poisonously hot and the steppe across which he had ridden, for all its golden beauty, its wealth of blue cornflour and yellow genista, had been wearisome. Overhead the sky was an unbroken bowl of blue and at its zenith rode a brazen merciless sun.

He took a leather cigar-case from his pocket, extracted a long black cheroot and lit it; then, leaving his horse to its own devices, he mounted the bank by the side of the road, from whence he could look across the valley of the Dneiper. That majestic river lay beneath him and to the right.

Before him, at the foot of the long, steep and winding road, lay the quarter which is called Podol.

For the rest his horizon was filled with a jumble of buildings, magnificent or squalid; the half-revealed roofs on the wooded slopes of the four hills, and the ragged fringe of belfry and glittering cupola which made up the picture of Kieff.

The month was June and the year of grace 1914, and Malcolm Hay, chief engineer of the Ukraine-American Oil Corporation, had no other thought in his mind, as he looked upon the undoubted beauty of Kieff, than that it would be a very pleasant place to leave. He climbed the broken stone wall and stood, his hands thrust deeply into his breeches pockets, watching the scene. It was one of those innumerable holy days which the Russian peasant celebrated with such zest. Rather it was the second of three consecutive feast days and, as Malcolm knew, there was small chance of any work being done on the field until his labourers had taken their fill of holiness, and had slept off the colossal drunk which inevitably followed this pious exercise.

A young peasant, wearing a sheepskin coat despite the stifling heat of the day, walked quickly up the hill leading a laden donkey. The man stopped when he was abreast of Malcolm, took a cigarette from the inside of his coat and lit it.

"God save you, *dudushka*," he said cheerfully.

Malcolm was so used to being addressed as "little grandfather," and that for all his obvious youth, that he saw nothing funny in the address.

"God save you, my little man," he replied.

The new-comer was a broad-faced, pleasant-looking fellow with a ready grin, and black eyebrows that met above his nose. Malcolm Hay knew the type, but to-day being for idleness, he did not dread the man's loquacity as he would had it been a working day.

"My name is Gleb," introduced the man: "I come from the village of Potchkoi where my father has seven cows and a bull."

"God give him prosperity and many calves," said Malcolm mechanically.

"Tell me, *gospodar*, do you ride into our holy city to-day?"

"Surely," said Malcolm.

"Then you will do well to avoid the Street of Black Mud," said Gleb.

Malcolm waited.

"I speak wisely because of my name," said the man with calm assurance; "possibly your excellence has wondered why I should bear the same name as the great saint who lies yonder," he pointed to one of the towering belfries shimmering with gold that rose above the shoulder of a distant hill. "I am Gleb, the son of Gleb, and it is said that we go back a thousand years to the Holy Ones. Also, it was prophesied by a wise woman," said the peasant, puffing out a cloud of smoke and crossing himself at the same time, "that I should go the way of holiness and that after my death my body should be incorruptible."

"All this is very interesting, little brother," said Malcolm with a smile, "but first you must tell me why I should not go into the Street of Black Mud."

The man laughed softly.

"Because of Israel Kensky," he said significantly.

You could not live within a hundred miles of Kieff and not know of Israel Kensky. Malcolm realized with a start that he had not met the old man since he left him in London.

"In what way has Israel Kensky offended?" asked Malcolm, understanding the menace in the man's tone.

Gleb, squatting in the dust, brushed his sheepskin delicately with the tips of his fingers.

"Little father," he said, "all men know Israel Kensky is a Jew and that he practises secret devil-rites, using the blood of Christian children.

This is the way of Jews, as your lordship knows. Also he was seen on the plains to shoot pigeons, which is a terrible offence, for to shoot a pigeon is to kill the Holy Ghost."

Malcolm knew that the greater offence had not yet been stated and waited.

"To-day I think they will kill him if the Grand Duke does not send his soldiers to hold the people in check—or the Grand Duchess, his lovely daughter who has spoken for him before, does not speak again."

"But why should they kill Kensky?" asked Malcolm.

It was not the first time that Israel Kensky had been the subject of hostile demonstrations. The young engineer had heard these stories of horrible rites practised at the expense of Christian children, and had heard them so often that he was hardened to the repetition.

The grin had left the man's face and there was a fanatical light in the solemn eyes when he replied:

"*Gospodar*, it is known that this man has a book which is called 'The Book of All-Power!'"

Malcolm nodded.

"So the foolish say," he said.

"It has been seen," said the other; "his own daughter, Sophia Kensky, who has been baptised in the faith of Our Blessed Lord, has told the Archbishop of this book. She, herself, has seen it."

"But why should you kill a man because he has a book?" demanded Malcolm, knowing well what the answer would be.

"Why should we kill him! A thousand reasons, *gospodar*," cried the man passionately; "he who has this book understands the black magic of Kensky and the Jews! By the mysteries in this book he is able to torment his enemies and bring sorrow to the Christians who oppose him. Did not the man Ivan Nickolovitch throw a stone at him, and did not Ivan drop dead the next day on his way to mass, aye and turn black before they carried him to the hospital? And did not Mishka Yakov, who spat at him, suffer almost immediately from a great swelling of the throat so that she is not able to speak or swallow to this very day without pain?"

Malcolm jumped down from the wall and laughed, and it was a helpless little laugh, the laugh of one who, for four long years, had fought against the superstitions of the Russian peasantry. He had seen the work of his hands brought to naught, and a boring abandoned just short of the oil because a cross-eyed man, attracted by curiosity, had come and looked at the work. He had seen his wells go up in smoke for some imaginary act of witchcraft on the part of his foreman, and, though he laughed, he was in no sense amused.

"Go with God, little brother," he said; "some day you will have more sense and know that men do not practise witchcraft."

"Perhaps I am wiser than you," said Gleb, getting up and whistling for his donkey, who had strayed up the side lane.

Before Malcolm could reply there was a clatter of hoofs and two riders came galloping round the bend of the road making for the town. The first of these was a girl, and the man who followed behind was evidently the servant of an exalted house, for he wore a livery of green and gold.

Gleb's ass had come cantering down at his master's whistle and now stood broadside-on in the middle of the road, blocking the way. The girl pulled up her horse with a jerk and, half-turning her head to her attendant, she called. The man rode forward.

"Get your donkey out of the way, fool," he boomed in a deep-chested roar.

He was a big man, broad-shouldered and stout. Like most Russian domestic servants, his face was clean-shaven, but Malcolm, watching the scene idly, observed only this about him—that he had a crooked nose and that his hair was a fiery red.

"Gently, gently." It was the girl who spoke and she addressed her restive horse in English.

As for Gleb, the peasant, he stood, his hands clasped before him, his head humbly hung, incapable of movement, and with a laugh Malcolm jumped down from the bank, seized the donkey by his bridle and drew him somewhat reluctantly to the side of the road. The girl's horse had been curveting and prancing nervously, so that it brought her to within a few paces of Malcolm, and he looked up, wondering what rich man's daughter was this who spoke in English to her horse. . . only once before had he seen her in the light of day.

The face was not pale, yet the colour that was in her cheeks so delicately toned with the ivory-white of forehead and neck that she looked pale. The eyes, set wide apart, were so deep a grey that in contrast with the creamy pallor of brow they appeared black.

A firm, red mouth he noticed; thin pencilling of eyebrows, a tangle of dark brown hair; but neither sight of her nor sound of her tired drawling voice, gave her such permanence in his mind as the indefinite sense of womanliness that clothed her like an aurora.

He responded wonderfully to some mysterious call she made upon the man in him. He felt that his senses played no part in shaping his view. If he had met her in the dark, and had neither seen nor heard; if she had been a bare-legged peasant girl on her way to the fields; if he had met her anywhere, anyhow—she would have been divine.

She, for her part, saw a tall young man, mahogany faced, leanly made, in old shooting-jacket and battered Stetson hat. She saw a good forehead and an unruly mop of hair, and beneath two eyes, now awe-stricken by her femininity (this she might have guessed) rather than by her exalted rank. They were eyes with a capacity for much laughter, she thought, and wished Russian men had eyes like those.

"My horse is afraid of your donkey, I think," she smiled.

"It isn't my donkey," he stammered, and she laughed again frankly at his embarrassment.

And then the unexpected happened. With a frightened neigh her horse leapt sideways toward him. He sprang back to avoid the horse's hoofs and heard her little exclamation of dismay. In the fraction of a second he realized she was falling and held out his arms to catch her. For a moment she lay on his breast, her soft cheek against his, the overpowering fragrance of her presence taking his breath away. Then she gently disengaged herself and stepped back. There was colour in her face now and something which might have been mischief, or annoyance, or sheer amusement, in her eyes.

"Thank you," she said.

Her tone was even and did not encourage further advances on his part.

"I lost my balance. Will you hold my horse's head?"

She was back in the saddle and turning, with a proud little inclination of her head, was picking a way down the steep hill before he realized what had happened. He gazed after her, hoping at least that feminine curiosity would induce her to turn and look back, but in this he was disappointed.

The peasant, Gleb, still stood by the side of the road, his hands clasped, his head bent as though in a trance.

"Wake up, little monkey," said Malcolm testily. "Why did you not hold the horse for the lady whilst I helped her to mount?"

"*Dudushka*, it is forbidden, *Zaprestcheno*," said the man huskily. "She is *Kaziomne*! The property of the Czar!"

"The Czar!" gasped Malcolm.

He had lived long enough in Russia to have imbibed some of the awe and reverence for that personage.

"Little master," said the man, "it was her Magnificence, the Grand Duchess Irene Yaroslav."

"The Grand——!" Malcolm gasped. The reality of his dreams and he had not recognized her!

Long after the peasant had departed he stood on the spot where he had held her, like a man in a trance, and he was very thoughtful when he picked up the reins of his horse and swung himself into the saddle.

Kieff is built upon many hills and it has the beauty and distinction of possessing steeper roads than any other city in Europe. He was on his way to the Grand Hotel, and this necessitated his passing through Podol, crossing the Hill of the Cliff, and descending into the valley beyond.

Considering it was a feast day the streets were strangely deserted. He met a few old men and women in festal garb and supposed that the majority of the people were at the shrines in which Kieff abounds. He passed through the poorer Jewish quarter, and did not remember the peasant's warning not to go into the Street of Black Mud until he had turned into that thoroughfare.

Long before he had reached the street he heard the roar of the crowd, and knew that some kind of trouble was brewing. The street was filled with knots of men and women, and their faces by common attraction, were turned in one direction. The focal point was a densely packed crowd which swayed toward the gateway of a tall, grim-looking house, which he recognized as the home of the millionaire, Kensky.

The roar intensified to a continuous shriek of malignant hate. He saw sticks and fists brandished and heard above the scream of frenzied women the deep-throated "Kill! Death to the Jew!" which was not unfamiliar to one who knew Kieff in moments of religious excitement. It was no business of his, and he drew his horse to the side of the street and watched, wondering what part the black-bearded Russian priests, who were in force and who seemed to form the centre of each knot of idlers, were playing in this act of persecution.

On the outskirts of the crowd he observed a green and gold coat, and, its wearer turning his head, he recognized him as the swarthy menial who had ridden behind the Grand Duchess. He was as violent and as energetic as the most lawless, and seemed engaged in pushing men into the crowd and dragging forward hesitant bystanders to swell the throng which was pressing about the iron gates of the building.

And then Malcolm saw something which brought his heart to his mouth, a white hand raised from above the bobbing black heads, a hand raised in appeal or command. Instinctively he knew its owner and spurred his horse into the throng, sending the people flying in all directions. There was a small clear space immediately before the door which enabled him to see the two chief actors in the drama long before he was within hailing distance.

The space was caused by a dead horse, as he afterwards discovered, but, for the moment, his eyes were fixed on the girl who stood with her back to the grille, shielding with her frail body a little old man, white-bearded and bent, who crouched behind her outstretched arms, his pale face streaming with blood. A broken key in the grille told the story of his foiled attempt to escape. Grimy hands clutched at Malcolm's knees as he drove through the press, a stone whistled past his ear and shrill voices uttered imprecations at the daring foreigner, but he swerved to left and right and made a way until the sight of the dead horse brought his frightened mount to a quivering standstill.

He leapt from the saddle and sprang to the girl's side, and to his amazement his appearance seemed to strike consternation into her heart.

"Why did you come? Get away as quickly as you can," she breathed. "Oh, you were mad to come here!"

"But—but you?" he said.

"They will not hurt me," she said rapidly. "It is the old man they want. Can you smash the lock and get him inside?"

"Give us the book, Jew," yelled a deep voice above the babel of sound. "Give us the book and you shall live! Lady! Magnificence! Make the old man give us the book!"

Malcolm took a flying kick at the gate and the lock yielded. He half lifted, half carried the old man and pushed inside, where another locked door confronted them.

"Have you a key?" demanded Malcolm hurriedly. "Quick!"

The old man felt in his pocket with trembling fingers and in doing so he crept behind his guardian. Malcolm now turned and faced the crowd.

"Come in, for God's sake," he called to the girl, but she shook her head.

"They will not hurt me," she said over her shoulder; "it is you!"

At that moment Malcolm felt something heavy slipped into the loose pocket of his jacket and a quivering voice, harsh with fear, whispered in his ear:

"Keep it, *gospodar*. To-morrow I will come for it at the Grand Hotel at the middle hour!"

The crowd was now surging forward and the girl was being pressed back into the little lobby by their weight. Suddenly the door opened with a crack and the old man slipped through.

"Come, come," he cried.

Malcolm leapt forward, clasped the girl about the waist and swung her behind him.

The shrieks of the crowd broke and a new note crept into the pandemonium of sound, a note of fear. From outside came a clatter of hoofs on the cobbled roadway. There was a flash of red and white pennons, the glitter of steel lances and a glimpse of bottle-green coats as half a sotnia of Cossacks swept the street clear.

They looked at one another, the girl and the man, oblivious to the appeal of hand and voice which the old man in the doorway was offering.

"I think you are very brave," said the girl, "or else very foolish. You do not know our Kieff people."

"I know them very well," he said grimly.

"It was equally foolish of me to interfere," she said quickly, "and I ought not to blame you. They killed my horse."

She pointed to the dead horse lying before the doorway.

"Where was your servant?" he asked, but she made no reply. He repeated the question, thinking she had not heard and being at some loss for any other topic of conversation.

"Let us go out," she said, ignoring the query, "we are safe now."

He was following her when he remembered the packet in his pocket and turned to the old man.

"Here is your——"

"No, no, no, keep it," whispered Israel Kensky. "They may come again to-night! My daughter told them that I was carrying it. May she roast!"

"What is it?" asked Malcolm curiously.

The old man's lips parted in a toothless smile.

"It is the 'Book of All-Power!'"

He blinked up at Malcolm, peering into his face expectantly. "They all desire it, *gospodar*, from the Grand Duke in his beautiful palace to the *moujik* in his cellar—they all desire my lovely book! I trust you with it for one night, *gospodar*, because you are English. Ah, well, you are not Russian. Guard it closely, for it holds the secret of tears and of happiness. You shall learn how to make men and women your slaves and how to turn people into Jews, and how to make men and women adore you, ai, ai! There are recipes for beauty in my book which make plain women lovely and old men young!"

Malcolm could only stare.

Chapter 8

The Grand Duke is Affable

The girl's voice called, and Malcolm left old Kensky without a word and went to her side. "Will you walk with me to my father's palace?" she said. "I do not think it is safe for you to be alone."

A semi-circle of mounted Cossacks surrounded them now, and the unfaithful Boolba (such was the servant's name, he learnt) was standing with an impassive face holding his horse's head.

"One of the soldiers will take your horse," she said. "Boolba, you will follow us."

Her voice was stern and she looked the man straight in the eyes, but he did not flinch.

"*Prikazeno*, Highness, it is ordered," he said simply.

She turned and walked the way she had come, turning into the big square followed by a small escort of Cossacks.

They walked in silence for some time, and it was the girl who first spoke.

"What do you think of Russia, Mr. Hay?" she asked.

He jerked his head round at her in surprise.

"You didn't know me on the hill," she laughed, "but I knew you! And there are not so many foreigners in the Kieff region that you should be unknown to the Grand Duke," she said, "and besides, you were at the reception which my father gave a year ago."

"I did not see your Highness there," said Malcolm. "I came especially——" he stopped short in confusion.

"That was probably because I was not visible," she replied dryly. "I have been to Cambridge for a year to finish my education."

"That is why your English is so good," he smiled.

"It's much better than your Russian," she said calmly. "You ought not to have said '*ukhoditzay*' to people—you only say that to beggars, and I think they were rather annoyed with you."

"I should imagine they were," he laughed; "but won't you tell me what happened to your servant? I thought I saw him on the outskirts of the crowd and the impression I formed was——" he hesitated.

"I shouldn't form impressions if I were you," she said hurriedly. "Here in Russia one ought not to puzzle one's head over such things. When you meet the inexplicable, accept it as such and inquire no further."

She was silent again, and when she spoke she was more serious.

"The Russian people always impress me as a great sea of lava, boiling and spluttering and rolling slowly between frail banks which we have built for them," said the girl.

"I often wonder whether those banks will ever break," said Malcolm quietly; "if they do——"

"Yes?"

"They will burn up Russia," said Malcolm.

"So I think," said the girl. "Father believes that the war——" she stopped short.

"The war?"

Malcolm had heard rumours so often of the inevitable war which would be fought to establish the hegemony of the Slav over Eastern Europe that the scepticism in his tone was pardonable. She looked at him sharply.

"You do not think there will be war?"

"One has heard so often," he began.

"I know, I know," she said, a little impatiently, and changed the subject.

They talked about the people, the lovable character of the peasants, the extraordinary depth of their religious faiths, their amazing superstitions, and suddenly Malcolm remembered the book in his pocket, and was about to speak of it, but stopped himself, feeling that, by so speaking, he was betraying the confidence of the old man who had entrusted his treasure to a stranger's care.

"What is this story of the book of Kensky?"

"'The Book of All-Power'?"

She did not smile as he had expected her to.

"Old Israel Kensky is a curious man," she said guardedly. "The people credit him with all sorts of powers which of course he does not possess. They believe he is a wizard, that he can bend people to his will. They say the most terrible things about the religious ceremonies over which he presides."

They were mounting the hill behind which lay the fashionable quarter of Kieff with its great stone palaces, its wonderful cherry gardens and broad avenues.

"I like old Kensky," she went on; "he sometimes comes to the palace to bring new silks—he is the greatest merchant in Little Russia. He even tells me his troubles—he has a terrible daughter: you have heard about her?"

"I thought she was rather good," said Malcolm humorously. "Isn't she a Christian?"

The girl shrugged her shoulders. Evidently her Grand Ducal Highness had no great opinion of Sophia Kensky's conversion.

The Grand Ducal palace was built in the Byzantine style and presented, from the broad carriage drive that led from the road, a confusion of roofs, windows and bastions, as though the designer had left the working out of his plan to fifty different architects, and each architect had interpreted the scheme of construction in his own way.

The Grand Duke was standing in the portico as they went through the gate, and came down the steps to meet them. He was a mild-looking man of medium height and wore pince-nez. Malcolm remembered that on the one occasion he had met his Highness he had been disappointed in his lack of personal grandeur.

"My child, my child!" said the Duke, coming to the girl with outstretched arms. "What a terrible misfortune! How came you to be mixed up in this matter? The commandant has just telephoned to me. I have called for his resignation. By St. Inokeste, I will not have the rabble breathing upon you! And this is the good gentleman who came to your rescue?"

He surveyed Malcolm with his cold blue eyes, but both glance and intonation lacked the cordiality which his words implied.

"I thank you. I am indeed grateful to you. You understand they would not have harmed the Grand Duchess, but this you could not know. As for the Jew——"

He became suddenly thoughtful. He had the air of a man wholly preoccupied in his secret thoughts and who now emerged from his shell under the greatest protest. To Malcolm it seemed that he resented even the necessity for communicating his thoughts to his own daughter.

"I am happy to have been of service to your Grand Ducal Highness," said Malcolm correctly.

"Yes, yes, yes," interrupted the Grand Duke nervously, "but you will stay and breakfast with me? Come, I insist, Mr.—er—er——"

"Mr. Hay, father," said the girl.

The conversation throughout was carried on in English, which was not remarkable, remembering that that was the family language of the Court.

"Yes, yes, yes, Mr. Hay, you must stay to breakfast. You have been very good, very noble, I am sure. Irene, you must persuade this gentleman." He held out his hand jerkily and Malcolm took it with a bow.

Then without another word or even so much as a glance at his daughter, the Grand Duke turned and hurried back into the palace, leaving Malcolm very astonished and a little uncomfortable.

The girl saw his embarrassment.

"My father does not seem to be very hospitable," she smiled, and once more he saw that little gleam of mischief in her eyes, "but I will give you a warmer invitation."

He spread out his hands in mock dismay and looked down at his untidy clothes.

"Your Highness is very generous," he said, "but how can I come to the Grand Duke's table like this?"

"You will not see the Grand Duke," she laughed; "father gives these invitations but never accepts them himself! He breakfasts in his own room, so if you can endure me alone——" she challenged.

He said nothing but looked much, and her eyes fell before his. All the time he was conscious that red-haired Boolba stood stiffly behind him, a spectator, yet, as Malcolm felt, a participant in this small affair of the breakfast invitation. She followed Malcolm's look and beckoned the man forward. He had already surrendered the horses to an orderly.

"Take the lord to a guest-room," she said in Russian, "and send a valet to attend to him."

"It is ordered," said the man, and with a nod, the girl turned and walked into the house, followed at a more leisurely pace by Malcolm and the man with the crooked nose.

Boolba led the way up a broad flight of stairs, carpeted with thick red pile, along a corridor pierced at intervals with great windows, to another corridor leading off and through a door which, from its dimensions, suggested the entrance to a throne-room, into a suite gorgeously furnished and resplendent with silver electroliers. It consisted of a saloon leading into a bedroom, which was furnished in the same exquisite taste. A further door led to a marble-tiled bathroom.

"Such luxury!" murmured Malcolm.

"Has the *gospodar* any orders?"

It was the solemn Boolba who spoke. Malcolm looked at him.

"Tell me this, Boolba," he said, falling into the familiar style of address which experience had taught him was the correct line to follow when dealing with Russian servants, "how came it that your mistress was alone before the house of Israel Kensky, the Jew, and you were on the outskirts of the crowd urging them on?"

If the man felt any perturbation at the bluntness of the question he did not show it.

"Kensky is a Jew," he said coolly; "on the night of the Pentecost he takes the blood of new-born Christian babies and sprinkles his money so that it may be increased in the coming year. This Sophia Kensky, his own daughter, has told me."

Malcolm shrugged his shoulders.

"You are no ignorant *moujik*, Boolba," he said contemptuously, "you have travelled with his Highness all over the world." (This was a shot at a venture, but apparently was not without justification.) "How can you, an educated man of the people, believe such rubbish?"

"He has a book, *gospodar*," said Boolba, "and we people who desire power would have that book, for it teaches men how they may command the souls of others, so that when they lift their little fingers, those who hate them best shall obey them."

Malcolm looked at him in astonishment.

"Do you believe this?"

For the first time a smile crossed the face of the man with the crooked nose. It was not a pleasant smile to see, for there was cunning in it and a measureless capacity for cruelty.

"Who knows all the miracles and wonders of the world?" he said. "My lord knows there is a devil, and has he not his angels on earth? It is best to be sure of these things, and we cannot be certain—until we have seen the book which the Jew gave to your lordship."

He paused a little before uttering the last sentence which gave his assertion a special significance. Malcolm eyed him narrowly.

"The Jew did not give me any book, Boolba," he said.

"I thought your lordship——"

"You thought wrongly," said Malcolm shortly.

Boolba bowed and withdrew.

The situation was not a particularly pleasant one. Malcolm had in his possession a book which men were willing to commit murder to obtain, and he was not at all anxious that his name should be associated with the practice of witchcraft.

It was all ridiculous and absurd, of course, but then in Russia nothing was so absurd that it could be lightly dismissed from consideration. He walked to the door and turned the key, then took from his pocket the thing which Israel Kensky had slipped in. It was a thick, stoutly bound volume secured by two brass locks. The binding was of yellow calf, and it bore the following inscription in Russian stamped in gold lettering:

"The Book of All-Power."

"Herein is the magic of power and the words and symbols which unlock the sealed hearts of men and turn their proud wills to water."

On the bottom left-hand corner of the cover was an inscription in Hebrew, which Malcolm could not read, but which he guessed stood for the birth-name of Israel Kensky. He turned the book over in his hand, and, curiosity overcoming him, he tried to force his thumb-nail into the marbled edge of the leaves that he might secure a glimpse of its contents. But the book was too tightly bound, and after another careful examination, he pulled off his coat and started to make himself presentable for breakfast.

The little meal was wholly delightful. Besides Malcolm and the girl there were present a faded Russian lady, whom he guessed was her official chaperon, and a sour-visaged Russian priest who ceremoniously blessed the food and was apparently the Grand Duke's household chaplain. He did not speak throughout the meal, and seemed to be in a condition of rapt contemplation.

But for all Malcolm knew there might have been a hundred people present—he had eyes and ears only for the girl. She had changed to a dark blue costume beneath which was a plain white silk blouse cut deeply at the neck.

He was struck by the fact that she wore no jewels, and he found himself rejoicing at the absence of rings in general and of one ring in particular.

Of course, it was all lunacy, sheer clotted madness, as he told himself, but this was a day to riot in illusions, for undreamt-of things had happened, and who could swear that the days of fairies had passed? To meet a dream-Irene on his way to Kieff was unlikely, to rescue her from an infuriated mob (for though they insisted that she was in no danger he was no less insistent that he rescued her, since this illusion was the keystone to all others), to be sitting at lunch with such a vision of youthful loveliness—all these things were sufficiently outside the range of probabilities to encourage the development of his dream in a comfortable direction.

"To-night," thought he, "I shall be eating a prosaic dinner at the Grand Hotel, and the Grand Duchess Irene Yaroslav will be a remote personage whom I shall only see in the picture papers, or possibly over the heads of a crowd on her way to the railway station."

And so he was outrageously familiar. He ceased to "Highness" her, laughed at her jokes and in turn provoked her to merriment. The meal came to an end too soon for him, but not too soon for the nodding dowager nor the silent, contemplating priest, who had worn through his period of saintly abstraction and had grown most humanly impatient.

The girl looked at her watch.

"Good gracious," she said, "it is four o'clock and I have promised to go to tennis." (Malcolm loathed tennis from that hour.)

He took his leave of her with a return to something of the old ceremonial.

"Your Grand Ducal Highness has been most gracious," he said, but she arrested his eloquence with a little grimace.

"Please, remember, Mr. Hay, that I shall be a Grand Ducal Highness for quite a long time, so do not spoil a very pleasant afternoon by being over-punctilious."

He laughed.

"Then I will call you——"

He came to a dead end, and the moment was embarrassing for both, though why a Grand Ducal Highness should be embarrassed by a young engineer she alone might explain.

Happily there arrived most unexpectedly the Grand Duke himself, and if his appearance was amazing, as it was to judge by the girl's face, his geniality was sensational.

He crossed the hall and gripped the young man's hand.

"You're not going, Mr. Hay?" he asked. "Come, come, I have been a very bad host, but I do not intend to let you go so soon! I have much that I want to talk to you about. You are the engineer in charge of the Ukraine Oil Field, is it not so? Excellent! Now, I have oil on my estate in the Urals but it has never been developed. . ."

He took the young man by the arm and led him through the big doors to the garden, giving him no chance to complete or decently postpone his farewell to the girl, who watched with undisguised amazement this staggering affability on the part of her parent.

Chapter 9

The Hand at the Window

An hour later she came from tennis, to find her father obviously bored almost to the point of tears, yet making an heroic attempt to appear interested in Malcolm's enthusiastic dissertation of the future of the oil industry. The Grand Duke rose gladly on her appearance, and handed him over.

"I have persuaded Mr. Hay to dine with us to-night, and I have sent to the hotel for his baggage. He is most entertaining, my little love, most entertaining. Persuade him to talk to you about—er—oil and things," and he hurriedly withdrew.

The girl sat down on the seat he had vacated.

"You're a most amazing person, Mr. Hay," she smiled.

"So I have been told," said Malcolm, as he filled a glass with tea from the samovar.

"You have also a good opinion of yourself, it seems," she said calmly.

"Why do you think I am amazing, anyway?" said he recklessly, returning to the relationships they had established at luncheon.

"Because you have enchanted my father," she said.

She was not smiling now, and a troubled little frown gathered on her brow.

"Please tell me your magic."

"Perhaps it is the book," he said jestingly.

"The book!" she looked up sharply. "What book?"

And then, as a light dawned on her, she rose to her feet.

"You have—you have Israel Kensky's book?" she whispered in horror.

He nodded.

"Here with you?"

"Yes, here," he slapped his pocket.

She sat down slowly and reached out her hand, and he thought it shook.

"I do not know who was the madder—Israel Kensky to give it to you or you to take it," she said. "This is the only house in Kieff where your life is safe, and even here——" She stopped and shook her head. "Of course, you're safe here," she smiled, "but I wish the book were somewhere else."

She made no further reference either to the amazing volume or to her father, and that night, when he came down to dinner, feeling more on level terms with royalty (though his dress-suit was four years old and his patent shoes, good enough for such mild society functions as came his way, looked horribly cracked and shabby), he dismissed the matter from his mind. The dinner party was a large one. There were two bishops, innumerable popes, several bejewelled women, an officer or two and the inevitable duenna. He was introduced to them all, but remembered only Colonel Malinkoff, a quiet man whom he was to meet again.

To his amazement he found that he had been seated in the place of honour, to the right of the Grand Duke, but he derived very little satisfaction from that distinction, since the girl was at the other end of the table.

She looked worried and her conversation, so far as he could hear, consisted of "yes" and "no" and conventional expressions of agreement with the views of her companions.

But the duke was loquacious, and at an early stage of the dinner the conversation turned on the riot of the morning. There was nothing remarkable in the conversation till suddenly the Grand Duke, without preliminary, remarked in a matter-of-fact tone:

"The danger is that Kensky may very well use his evil powers against the welfare of Holy Church."

There was a murmur of agreement from the black-bearded popes, and Malcolm opened his eyes in astonishment.

"But surely your Highness does not believe that this man has any supernatural gift."

The Grand Duke stared at him through his glasses.

"Of course," he said, "if there are miracles of the Church why should there not be performed miracles by the Powers of Darkness? Here in Kieff," he went on, "we have no reason to doubt that miracles are performed every day. Who doubts that worship at the shrine of St. Barbara in the Church of St. Michael of the Golden Head protects us against lightning?"

"That is undoubtedly the fact, your Imperial Highness," said a stout pope, speaking with his mouth full. "I have seen houses with lightning conductors struck repeatedly, and I have never known any place to be touched by lightning if the master of the house was under the protection of St. Barbara."

"And beneath the Church of Exaltation," the Grand Duke went on, "more miracles have been performed than elsewhere in the world."

He peered round the table for contradiction.

"It was here that the Two Brothers are buried and it was their prayer that they should sleep together in the same grave. One died before the other, and when the second had passed away and they carried his body to the tomb, did not the body of the first brother arise to make room? And is there not a column in the catacomb to which, if a madman is bound, he recovers his reason? And are there not skulls which exude wonderful oils which cure men of the most terrible diseases, even though they are on the point of death?"

Malcolm drew a long breath. He could understand the superstitious reverence of the peasant for these relics and miracles, but these were educated men. One of them stood near to the throne and was versed in the intricacies of European diplomacy. These were no peasants steeped in ignorance, but intellectuals. He pinched himself to make sure that he was awake as the discussion grew and men swopped miracles in much the same spirit of emulation as store-loafers swop lies. But the conversation came back to him, led thereto by the Grand Duke, and once more it centred on that infernal book. The volume in question was not six inches from the Grand Duke, for Malcolm had stuffed it into his tail pocket before he came down to dinner, and this fact added a certain piquancy to the conversation.

"I do not doubt, your Highness," said a stout bishop, who picked his teeth throughout the dinner, "that Kensky's book is identical with a certain volume on devil worship which the blessed Saint Basil publicly denounced and damned. It was a book especially inspired by Satan, and contained exact rules, whereby he who practised the magic could bind in earthly and immortal obedience the soul of anybody he chose, thus destroying in this life their chance of happiness and in the life to come their souls' salvation."

All within reach of the bishop's voice crossed themselves three times.

"It would have been well," mused the Grand Duke, "if the people had succeeded this morning."

He shot a glance at Malcolm, a glance full of suspicious inquiry, but the young man showed no sign either of resentment or agreement. But he was glad when the dinner ended and the chance came to snatch a few words with the girl. The guests were departing early, and kummel and coffee was already being served on a large silver salver by the *buffetschek*, whom Malcolm recognized as the ubiquitous Boolba.

"I shall not see you again," said the girl in a low voice. "I am going to my room. But I want you to promise me something, Mr. Hay."

"The promise is made before you ask," said he.

"I want you to leave as early as you possibly can to-morrow morning for your mine, and if I send you word I want you to leave Russia without delay."

"But this is very astonishing."

She faced him squarely, her hands behind her back.

"Mr. Hay," she said, and her low voice was vibrant with feeling, "you have entangled yourself in an adventure which cannot possibly end well for you. Whatever happens, you cannot come out with credit and safety, and I would rather you came out with credit."

"I don't understand you," he said.

"I will make it plainer," said she. "Unless something happens in the next month or two which will point the minds of the people to other directions, you will be suspect. The fact that you have the book is known."

"I know," he said.

"By whom?" she asked quickly.

"By Boolba, your servant."

She raised her hand to her lips, as if to suppress a cry. It was an odd little trick of hers which he had noticed before.

"Boolba," she repeated. "Of course! That explains!"

At that moment the Grand Duke called him. The guests had dwindled away to half a dozen.

"Your coffee, Mr. Hay, and some of our wonderful Russian kummel. You will not find its like in any other part of the world."

Malcolm drank the coffee, gulped down the fiery liqueur, and replaced the glass on the tray. He did not see the girl again, and half an hour later he went up to his room, locked the door and undressed himself slowly, declining the assistance which had been offered to him by the trained valet.

From the open window came the heavy perfume of heliotrope, but it was neither the garden scent nor the moderate quantity of wine he had taken, nor the languid beauty of the night, which produced this delicious sensation of weariness. He undressed and got into his pyjamas, then sat at the end of his bed, his head between his hands.

He had sat for a long time like this, before he realized the strangeness of his attitude and getting on to his feet, found himself swaying.

"Doped," he said, and sat down again.

There was little of his brain that was awake, but that little he worked hard. He had been drugged. It was either in the kummel or in the coffee. Nothing but dope would make him feel as he was feeling now. He fell into bed and pulled the clothes about him. He wanted to keep awake to fight off the effects of the stuff and, by an absurd perversion of reasoning, he argued that he was in a more favourable position to carry out his plan if he made himself comfortable in bed, than if he followed any other course.

The drug worked slowly and erratically. He had moments of complete unconsciousness with intervals which, if they were not free from the effect of the agent, were at least lucid. One such interval must have come after he had been in bed for about an hour, for he found himself wide awake and lay listening to the thumping of his heart, which seemed to shake the bed.

The room was bathed in a soft green light, for it was a night of full moon. He could see dimly the furniture and the subdued gleam of silver wall-sconce, that caught the ghostly light and gave it a more mysterious value. He tried to rise but could not. To roll his head from side to side seemed the limitation of conscious effort.

And whilst he looked, the door opened noiselessly and closed again. Somebody had come into the room, and that somebody passed softly across the foot of the bed, and stood revealed against the window. Had he been capable of speech he would have cried out.

It was the girl!

He saw her plainly in a moment. She wore a wrapper over her nightdress, and carried a small electric lamp in her hand. She went to the chair where he had thrown his clothes and made a search. He saw her take something out and put it under her wrap, then she went back the way she came, pausing for the space of a second at the foot of his bed.

She stood there undecidedly, and presently she came up to the side of the bed and bent down over him. His eyes were half closed; he had neither the power of opening or shutting them, but he could see clearly the white hand that rested on the bed and the book that it held, and the polished table by the bedside reflecting the moonlight back to her face so that she seemed something as intangible and as shadowy as the night itself.

A little smile played upon her pale face, and every whispered word she uttered was clear and distinct.

"Good-bye, poor Mr. Hay," she said softly.

She shook her head as though in pity; then, stopping swiftly, she kissed him on the cheek and passed quickly to the half-open door by which she had entered. She was nearing the door when she stopped dead and shrank back toward the bed. Another electric lamp gleamed unexpectedly. He saw the white of her nightdress show as a dazzling strip of light where the beam caught it. Then the unknown intruder touched on the light, and they stood revealed, the girl tall, imperious, a look of scorn on her beautiful face, and the stout menial with the crooked nose.

Boolba wore an old dressing-gown girdled about with a soiled rainbow sash. His feet were bare, and in his two hands laying from palm to palm was a long thin knife.

At the sight of the girl he fell back, a grotesque sprawling movement which was not without its comicality. A look of blank bewilderment creased his big face.

"You—you, Highness!" he croaked. "The Jew, where is he?"

She was silent. Malcolm saw the quick rise and fall of her bosom, saw the book clutched closer to her side beneath the filmy silken gown.

Boolba looked from the girl to Malcolm, from Malcolm to the heavy curtains at either side of the open window—curtains which the drugged man had not drawn.

"He has left his quarters, Highness," Boolba spoke eagerly; "he was seen to enter the grounds of the palace—where is he?"

He took a step toward her.

"Stand back—you slave!" she breathed, but with a bound he was upon her. There was a brief struggle, and the book was wrenched from her hand.

Malcolm saw all this, but lay as one dead. He was conscious but paralysed by the potion, and could only watch the girl in the grip of the obese monster and feel his heart going like a steam hammer.

Boolba stood gloating over his prize, fondling the book in his big, coarse hands. Malcolm wondered why the girl did not scream—yet how could she? She was in his room in the middle of the night, she, a daughter of emperors.

The man tried to wrench open the locks which held the covers, but failed. Suddenly he looked up, and glared across at the girl.

He said nothing, but the suspicion in that scowl was emphasized when he moved to the wall near the window and the light of a bracket lamp.

Again he examined the book and for the first time spoke:

"Oh, Highness, was it you who sent for Israel Kensky that the book should be restored——"

So far he got when an arm came from behind the curtain—a hand blue-veined, and it held a yellow handkerchief.

The girl saw it, and her hand went to her mouth.

Then the handkerchief struck full across Boolba's face, covering it from forehead to the mouth.

For a moment the man was paralysed, then he pulled the handkerchief away and clawed at the clay-like substance which adhered to his face.

"Mother of God!"

He screamed the words and, dropping the book, stumbled forward, rubbing at his face, shrieking with pain.

The girl ran swiftly through the open door, for feet were now pattering along the corridors and the flicker of lights showed through the doorway. Boolba was rolling on the ground in agony when the servants crowded in, followed by the Grand Duke—and he alone was fully dressed.

"Boolba—what is it?"

"The book—the book! It is mine! See. . . floor!"

But the book had disappeared.

"Where, Boolba—where, my good Boolba?" The voice of Boolba's master was tremulous. "Show me—did he strike you—he shall suffer, by the saints! Look for it, Boolba!"

"Look! Look!" yelled the writhing man. "How shall I look? I who am blind—blind—blind!"

Chapter 10

Terror in Making

In the spring of 1919 Malcolm Hay came out from the Kursky Voksal carrying his own well-worn valise. An indifferent cigar was clenched between his white teeth, and there was a sparkle of amusement in his grave eyes. He stood seventy inches in his stockings, and an excellent judge of men who looked him over, noted the set and width of shoulders, the upward lift of chin, the tanned face and flexibility of body, marked him down "soldier"—either American or English.

Malcolm looked up and down the deserted street and then caught the eye of the solitary *intooski*, a thoughtful-looking man with a short, square beard, looking monstrously stout in his padded green coat, the livery of the Moscow drosky driver.

The man on the sidewalk smiled and walked across the pavement.

"Little brother," he said in fluent Russian, "would you condescend to drive me to the Hotel du Bazar Slav?"

The driver who had noted so approvingly the shape of Malcolm's shoulders did not immediately answer; then:

"British?—I thought you were."

He spoke excellent English, and Malcolm looked up at him bewildered.

"I seem to know your face, too—let me think."

The cab-driver tapped his bearded chin.

"I have it—Hay. I met you four years ago at a dinner party in Kieff—you are the manager of an oil company or something of the sort."

"Right," said the astonished young man, "but—I don't exactly place you."

The drosky driver smiled.

"And yet I dined with you," he said. "I sat next the Grand Duchess Irene—later, when war broke out, I invited you to my headquarters."

"Good God!" Malcolm's jaw dropped. "General Malinkoff!"

"Commanding the 84th Caucasian Division," said the bearded man dryly, "and now commanding one little horse. If you will get into my excellent cab I will drive you to a restaurant where we may eat and drink and be almost merry for—fifty roubles."

Malcolm stepped into the little drosky like a man in a dream. Malinkoff! He remembered him, a fine figure on a horse, riding through Kieff at the head of a glittering throng of staff officers. There was a function at the Grand Hotel to meet the new Commander, a great parade at that ancient palace in his honour—Malcolm had come in from the oil-fields partly to meet him at dinner—partly for news of one who had of a sudden vanished from his life.

The drosky drove furiously through the east end of the town, and the passenger noted that the driver was careful to avoid the big thoroughfares which led to the Krasnaya Plotzad and that centre of Moscow which is the Kremlin.

Presently it drew up before a small eating-house in a poor street, and the driver hoisted himself to the ground. He left his horse unattended and, leading the way, pushed open the swing doors of the restaurant and passed down a long, low-ceilinged room crowded with diners, to a table at the far end.

"Sit down, Mr. Hay. I can promise you a fair but by no means sybarite feast—good morning, Nicholas Vassilitsky."

He nodded pleasantly to a grey-haired man in a workman's blouse sitting at the next table, and the man addressed rose stiffly, bowed and sat down.

"If you wish your clothes valeted whilst you are in Moscow, I recommend my friend," said the driver, snapping his fingers towards a stout waitress. "Colonel Nicholas Vassilitsky is not only an excellent Director of Military Intelligence but he can press a pair of trousers with any man."

He gave his orders briefly, and turned to his companion.

"First of all, let me interrogate you. You are on your way to Petrograd?"

"Yes—I am on my way home. During the war I have been controlling allied supplies in Little Russia—the Revolution stopped that."

"Fortunate man—to have a country," said General Malinkoff, and he spoke seriously and without bitterness. "A country and an army—coherent, disciplined comrades in arms."

He shrugged his padded shoulders.

"Yes—you are on your way to your home? It will take you months to leave the country—if you ever leave it. I tried to leave last month. I am a reactionary with a leaning toward discipline. I cannot breathe the air of democracy. I used to think I had Liberal ideas. There was a time when I thought that a day would dawn when the world would be a great United States of Free People. Ah, well—I am still a reactionary."

Malcolm knew that behind those grave eyes was a world of laughter, that beneath the solemn words was a gentle irony, and yet for the while he could not distinguish how much of tragedy there was in the man's fun.

"But why are you——"

"Driving a cab?" The general finished the sentence. "Because, my friend, I am human. I must eat, for example; I must have a room to sleep in. I need cigarettes, and clean shirts at least three times a week—for God's sake never let that be known. I must also have warm clothes for the winter—in fact, I must live."

"But haven't you—money?" Malcolm felt all a decent man's embarrassment. "Forgive me butting into your affairs, but naturally I'm rather hazed."

"Naturally," laughed the general. "A bottle of kavass, my peach of Turkistan, and a glass for our comrade."

"Long live the Revolution!" wheezed the waitress mechanically.

"Long may it live, little mother!" responded the general.

When the girl had gone he squared round to his companion.

"I have no shame, Mr. Hay—I'm going to let you pay for your own dinner because I cannot in these democratic times pauperize you by paying for you. No, I have no money. My balance in the State bank has been confiscated to the sacred cause of the people. My estate, a hundred versts or so from Moscow, confiscated to the sacred cause of the Revolution, my house in Petrograd is commandeered to the sacred service of the Soviet."

"But your command?"

The general did not smile now. He laid down his knife and fork and threw a glance behind him.

"The men began shooting their officers in March, 1917," he said, lowering his voice. "They executed the divisional staff in May—the democratic spirit was of slow growth. They spared me because I had written a book in my youth urging popular government and had been confined in the fortess of Vilna for my crime. When the army was disbanded I came to Moscow, and the cab was given to me by a former groom of mine, one Isaac Mosservitch, who is now a judge of the high court and dispenses pretty good law, though he cannot sign his own name."

"Mr. Hay," he went on earnestly, "you did wrong to come to Moscow. Get back to Kieff and strike down into the Caucasus. You can reach the American posts outside of Tiflis. You'll never leave Russia. The

Bolsheviks have gone mad—blood-mad, murder-mad. Every foreigner is suspect. The Americans and the English are being arrested. I can get you a passport that will carry you to Odessa, and you can reach Batoum, and Baku from there."

Malcolm leant back in his chair and looked thoughtfully at the other. "Is it so bad?"

"Bad! Moscow is a mad-house. Listen—do you hear anything?"

Above the hum of conversation Malcolm caught a sound like the cracking of whips.

"Rifle-firing," said the general calmly. "There's a counter-revolution in progress. The advanced Anarchists are in revolt against the Bolsheviks. There is a counter-revolution every morning. We cab-drivers meet after breakfast each day and decide amongst ourselves which of the streets shall be avoided. We are pretty well informed—Prince Dalgoursky, who was a captain in the Preopojensky Guard, sells newspapers outside the Soviet headquarters, and the comrades give him tips. One of these days the comrades will shoot him, but for the moment he is in favour, and makes as much as a hundred roubles a day."

The waitress came to the table, and the conversation momentarily ceased. When she had gone Malcolm put the question which he had asked so often in the past four years.

"Can you give me any news of the Grand Duke Yaroslav?"

The other shook his head.

"His Highness was in Petrograd when I heard of him last."

"And—and his daughter? She has been with the Russian Red Cross on the Riga front, I know."

The bearded man shot a queer glance at his companion.

"In what circumstances did you see her last?" he asked.

Malcolm hesitated.

He could hardly tell a stranger of that tragic scene which was enacted in his bedroom. From the moment she had fled through the door he had not set eyes upon her. In the morning when he had wakened, feeling sick and ill, he had been told that the Grand Duke and his daughter had left by the early northern express for the capital. Of Boolba, that hideously blinded figure, he heard nothing. When he inquired for Israel Kensky, men shrugged and said that he had "disappeared." His house was closed and the old man might be in prison or in hiding. Later he was to learn that Kensky had reappeared in Moscow, apparently without hindrance from the authorities. As for Boolba, he had kept his counsel.

"You seem embarrassed," smiled Malinkoff. "I will tell you why I ask. You know that her Grand Ducal Highness was banished from Court for disobedience to the royal will?"

Malcolm shook his head.

"I know nothing—absolutely nothing. Kieff and Odessa are full of refugees and rumours, but one is as much a suspect as the other."

"She would not marry—that is all. I forget the name of the exalted personage who was chosen for her, though I once helped to carry him up to bed—he drank heavily even in those days. God rest him! He died like a man. They hung him in a sack in Peter and Paul, and he insulted the Soviets to the last!"

"So—so she is not married?"

The general was silent, beckoning the waitress.

"My little dear," he said, "what shall I pay you?"

She gave him the scores and they settled.

"Which way now?" asked the general.

"I hardly know—what must a stranger do before he takes up his abode?"

"First find an abode," said the general with a meaning smile. "You asked me to drive you to the Hotel Bazar Slav, my simple but misguided friend! That is a Soviet headquarters. You will certainly go to a place adjacent to the hotel to register yourself, and afterwards to the Commissary to register all over again, and, if you are regarded with approval, which is hardly likely, you will be given a ticket which will enable you to secure the necessities of life—the tickets are easier to get than the food."

The first call at the house near the Bazar Slav gave them neither trouble nor results. The Soviet headquarters was mainly concerned with purely administrative affairs, and the organization of its membership. Its corridors and doorway were crowded with soldiers wearing the familiar red armlet, and when Malinkoff secured an interview with a weary looking and unkempt official, who sat collarless in his shirt sleeves at a table covered with papers, that gentleman could do no more than lean back in his chair and curse the interrupters volubly.

"We might have dispensed with the headquarters visit," said Malinkoff, "but it is absolutely necessary that you should see the Commissary unless you want to be pulled out of your bed one night and shot before you're thoroughly awake. By the way, we have an interesting American in gaol—by his description I gather he is what you would call a gun-man."

Malcolm stared.

"Here—a gun-man?"

Malinkoff nodded.

"He held up the Treasurer-General of the Soviet and relieved him of his wealth. I would like to have met him—but I presume he is dead. Justice is swift in Moscow, especially for those who hold up the officials of the Revolution."

"What sort of justice do these people administer?" asked Malcolm curiously.

Malinkoff shrugged his padded shoulders.

"Sometimes I think that the very habit of justice is dead in this land," he said. "On the whole they are about as just and fair as was the old regime—that is not saying much, is it? The cruelty of our rule to-day is due rather to ignorance than to ill will. A few of the men higher up are working off their old grievances and are profiting enormously, but the rank and file of the movement are labouring for the millennium."

"I think they're mad," said Malcolm.

"All injustice is mad," replied Malinkoff philosophically. "Now get into my little cab, and I will drive you to the Commissary."

The Commissary occupied a large house near the Igerian Gate. It was a house of such noble proportions that at first Malcolm thought it was one of the old public offices, and when Malinkoff had drawn up at the gate he put the question.

"That is the house of the Grand Duke Yaroslav," said Malinkoff quietly. "I think you were inquiring about him a little earlier in the day."

The name brought a little pang to Malcolm's heart, and he asked no further questions. There was a sentry on the *podyasde*—an untidy, unshaven man, smoking a cigarette—and a group of soldiers filled the entrance, evidently the remainder of the guard.

The Commissary was out. When would he be back? Only God knew. He had taken "the Little Mother" for a drive in the country, or perhaps he had gone to Petrograd—who knew? There was nobody to see but the Commissary—on this fact they insisted with such vehemence that Malcolm gathered that whoever the gentleman was, he brooked no rivals and allowed no possible supplanter to stand near his throne.

They came back at four o'clock in the afternoon, but the Commissary was still out. It was nine o'clock, after five inquiries, that the sentry replied "Yes" to the inevitable question.

"Now you will see him," said Malinkoff, "and the future depends upon the potency of your favourite patron saint."

Malcolm stopped in the doorway.

"General——" he said.

"Not that word," said Malinkoff quickly. "Citizen or comrade—comrade for preference."

"I feel that I am leading you into danger—I have been horribly selfish and thoughtless. Will it make any difference to you, your seeing him?"

Malinkoff shook his head.

"You're quite right, it is always dangerous to attract the attention of the Committee for Combatting the Counter-Revolution," he said, "but since I have taken you in hand I might as well see him as stay outside on my cab, because he is certain to inquire who brought you here, and it might look suspicious if I did not come in with you. Besides, somebody will have to vouch for you as a good comrade and friend of the Soviet."

He was half in earnest and half joking, but wholly fatalistic.

As they went up the broad spiral staircase which led to the main floor of the Yaroslav Palace, Malcolm had qualms. He heartily cursed himself for bringing this man into danger. So far as he was concerned, as he told himself, there was no risk at all, because he was a British traveller, having no feeling one way or the other toward the Soviet Government. But Malinkoff would be a marked man, under suspicion all the time. Before the office of the Commissary was a sentry without rifle. He sat at a table which completely blocked the doorway, except for about eight inches at one side. He inquired the business of the visitors, took their names and handed them to a soldier, and with a sideways jerk of his head invited them to squeeze past him into the bureau.

Chapter 11

THE COMMISSARY WITH THE CROOKED NOSE

There were a dozen men in the room in stained military overcoats and red armlets. One, evidently an officer, who carried a black portfolio under his arm, was leaning against the panelled wall, smoking and snapping his fingers to a dingy white terrier that leapt to his repeated invitations.

At the table, covered with documents, were two people, the man and the woman.

She, sprawling indolently forward, her head upon her arm, her strong brown face turned to the man, was obviously a Jewess. The papers were streaked and greasy where her thick black ringlets had rested, and the ashes of her cigarette lay in little untidy heaps on the table.

The man was burly, with a great breadth of shoulder and big rough hands. But it was his face which arrested the feet of Malcolm and brought him to a sudden halt the moment he came near enough to see and recognize the Commissary.

It was not by his bushy red beard nor the stiff, upstanding hair, but by the crooked nose, that he recognized Boolba, sometime serving-man to the Grand Duke Yaroslav. Malcolm, looking at the sightless eyes, felt his spine go creepy.

Boolba lifted his head sharply at the sound of an unfamiliar footfall.

"Who is this?" he asked. "Sophia Kensky, you who are my eyes, tell me who is this?"

"Oh, a boorjoo," said the woman lazily.

"A foreigner too—who are you, boorjoo?"

"A Britisher," said Malcolm.

Boolba lifted his chin and turned his face at the voice.

"A Britisher," he repeated slowly. "The man on the oil-fields. Tell me your name."

"Hay—Malcolm Hay," said Malcolm, and Boolba nodded.

His face was like a mask and he expressed no emotion.

"And the other?"

"Malinkoff!" snapped the voice at Malcolm's side, and Boolba nodded.

"Commanding an army—I remember. You drive a cab, comrade. Are there any complaints against this man?"

He turned his face to Sophia Kensky, and she shook her head.

"Are there any complaints against this man, Sophia?" he repeated.

"None that I know. He is an aristocrat and a friend of the Romanoffs."

"Huh!" The grunt sounded like a note of disappointment. "What do you want?"

"The stranger wishes permission to remain in Moscow until he can find a train to the north," said Malinkoff.

Boolba made no reply. He sat there, his elbows on the table, his fingers twining and untwining the thick red hair of his beard.

"Where does he sleep to-night?" he asked after awhile.

"He sleeps in my stable, near the Vassalli Prospekt," said Malinkoff.

Boolba turned to the woman, who was lighting a new cigarette from the end of the old one, and said something in a low, growling tone.

"Do as you wish, my little pigeon," she said audibly.

Again his hand went to his beard and his big mouth opened in meditation. Then he said curtly:

"Sit down."

There was no place to sit, and the two men fell back amongst the soldiers.

Again the two at the table consulted, and then Sophia Kensky called a name. The man in a faded officer's uniform came forward, his big black portfolio in his hand, and this he laid on the table, opening the flap and taking out a sheaf of papers.

"Read them to me, Sophia," said Boolba. "Read their names."

He groped about on the table and found first a rubber stamp and then a small, flat ink-pad. Sophia lifted the first of the papers and spelt out the names.

"Mishka Sasanoff," she said, and the man growled.

"An upstart woman and very ugly," he said. "I remember her. She used to whip her servants. Tell me, Sophia, my life, what has she done now?"

"Plotted to destroy the Revolution," said the woman.

"Huh!" grunted the man, as he brought his rubber stamp to the paper, passing it across to the waiting officer, who replaced it in his portfolio. "And the next?"

"Paul Geslkin," she said and passed the document to him. "Plotting to overthrow the Revolution."

"A boorjoo, a tricky young man, in league with the priests," he said, and again his stamp came down upon the paper, and again the paper went across the table into the portfolio of the officer.

The soldiers about Malcolm and his friend had edged away, and they were alone.

"What are these?" whispered Malcolm.

"Death warrants," replied Malinkoff laconically, and for the second time a cold chill ran down Malcolm's spine.

Name after name were read out, and the little rubber stamp, which carried death to one and sorrow to so many, thudded down upon the paper. Malcolm felt physically ill. The room was close and reeked of vile tobacco fumes. There was no ventilation, and the oil lamps made the apartment insufferably hot. An hour, two hours passed, and no further notice was paid to the two men.

"I can't understand it quite," said Malinkoff in a low voice. "Ordinarily this would mean serious trouble, but if the Commissary had any suspicion of you or me, we should have been in prison an hour ago."

Then suddenly Boolba rose.

"What is the hour?" he said.

A dozen voices replied.

"Half-past ten? It is time that the sweeper was here."

He threw back his head and laughed, and the men joined in the laughter. With a great yellow handkerchief, which reminded Malcolm of something particularly unpleasant, Boolba wiped the streams from his sightless eyes and bent down to the woman at his side, and Malcolm heard him say: "What is his name—he told me," and then he stood up.

"Hay," he said, "you are a boorjoo. You have ordered many men to sweep your room. Is not good that a house should be clean, eh?"

"Very good, Boolba," said Malcolm quietly.

"Boolba he calls me. He remembers well. That is good! I stood behind him, comrades, giving wine and coffee and bowing to this great English lord! Yes, I, Boolba!" he struck his chest, "crawled on my knees to this man, and he calls me Boolba now—Boolba!" he roared ferociously. "Come here! Do this! Clean my boots, Boolba! Come, little Boolba, bow thy neck that I may rest my foot!"

A voice from the door interrupted him.

"Good!" he said. "My sweeper has arrived, Hay. Once a day she sweeps my room and once a day she makes my bed. No ordinary woman will satisfy Boolba. She must come in her furs, drive in her fine carriage from the Nijitnkaya—behold!"

Malcolm looked to the doorway and was struck dumb with amazement.

The girl who came in was dressed better than he expected any woman to be dressed in Moscow. A sable wrap was about her shoulders, a sable toque was on her head. He could not see the worn shoes nor the shabby dress beneath the costly furs; indeed, he saw nothing but the face—the face of his dreams—unchanged, unlined, more beautiful than he had remembered her. She stood stiffly in her pride, her little chin held up, her contemptuous eyes fixed upon the man at the table. Then loosing her wrap, she hung it upon a peg, and opening a cupboard, took out a broad broom.

"Sweep, Irene Yaroslav," said the man.

Malcolm winced at the word, and Malinkoff turned to him sharply.

"You know her?" he said. "Of course you do—I remember. Was that why Boolba kept us waiting?"

"He was butler in the Yaroslav household," said Malcolm in the same tone.

"That explains it," said Malinkoff. "All this is for the humiliation of the Grand Duchess."

"Sweep well, little one," scoffed Boolba from his table. "Does it not do your heart good, Sophia Kensky? Oh, if I had only eyes to see! Does she go on her knees? Tell me, Sophia."

But the woman found no amusement in the sight, and she was not smiling. Her high forehead was knitted, her dark eyes followed every movement of the girl. As Boolba finished speaking she leant forward and demanded harshly:

"Irene Yaroslav, where is Israel Kensky?"

"I do not know," replied the girl, not taking her eyes from her work.

"You lie," said the woman. "You shall tell me where he is and where he has hidden his 'Book of All-Power.' She knows, Boolba."

"Peace, peace!" he said, laying his big hand on her shoulder. "Presently she will tell and be glad to tell. Where is your father, Irene Yaroslav?"

"You know best," she replied, and the answer seemed to afford him amusement.

"He was a religious man," he scoffed. "Did he not believe in miracles? Was there any saint in Kieff he did not patronize? He is with the saints this day," and then, in a fierce whisper to Sophia—"How did she look? Tell me, Sophia. How did she look when I spoke?"

"He died three weeks ago," said Irene quietly, "at the Fortress of Peter and Paul," and Boolba rapped out an oath.

"Who told you? Who told you?" he roared. "Tell me who told you, and I will have his heart out of him! I wanted to tell you that myself!"

"The High Commissary Boyaski," she replied, and Boolba swallowed his rage, for who dared criticize the High Commissaries, who hold power of life and death in their hands, even over their fellow officials? He sank down in his chair again and turned impatiently to Sophia.

"Have you no tongue in your head, Sophia Kensky!" he asked irritably. "Tell me all she does. How is she sweeping—where?"

"By the men, near the big bookcase," said the woman reluctantly.

"Yes, yes," and he nodded his great head.

He rose, walked round the table, and paced slowly to the girl as she stood quietly waiting. Malcolm had no weapon in his pocket. He had been warned by Malinkoff that visitors were searched. But on the table lay a sheathed sword—possibly the mark of authority which Boolba carried. But evidently this ceremony was a nightly occurrence. Boolba did no more than pass his hand over the girl's face.

"She is cool," he said in a disappointed tone. "You do not work hard enough, Irene Yaroslav. To-morrow you shall come with water and shall scrub this room."

The girl made no reply, but as he walked back to his seat of authority she continued her work, her eyes fixed on the floor, oblivious of her surroundings. Presently she worked round the room until she came to where Malcolm stood, and as she did so for the first time she raised her head, and her eyes met his. Again he saw that little trick of hers; her hand went to her mouth, then her head went down, and she passed on as though she had never seen him.

"What did she do, Sophia? Tell me what she did when she came to the Englishman. Did she not see him?"

"She was startled," grumbled Sophia; "that is all. Boolba, let the woman go."

"Nay, nay, my little pigeon, she must finish her work."

"She has finished," said Sophia impatiently; "how long must this go on, Boolba? Is she not an aristocrat and a Romanoff, and are there none of your men who want wives?"

Malcolm felt rather than saw the head of every soldier in the room lift to these words.

"Wait a little," said Boolba. "You forget the book, my little pigeon—the 'Book of All-Power.' I would have that rather than that Irene Yaroslav found a good husband from our comrades. You may go, Irene Yaroslav," he said. "Serge!"

The officer who had taken the death warrants, and who stood waiting for dismissal, came forward.

"Take our little brother Malinkoff and the Britisher Hay and place them both in the prison of St. Basil. They are proved enemies to the Revolution."

"I wonder who will feed my little horse to-night," said Malinkoff as, handcuffed to his companion, he marched through the streets in the light of dawn, en route, as he believed, to certain death.

Chapter 12

IN THE PRISON OF ST. BASIL

The temporary prison called by Boolba "St. Basil," was made up of four blocks of buildings. All save one were built of grey granite, and presented, when seen from the courtyard below, tiers of little windows set with monotonous regularity in discoloured walls. The fourth was evidently also of granite, but at some recent period an attempt had been made to cover its forbidding facade with plaster. The workmen had wearied of their good intent and had left off when their labours were half finished, which gave the building the gruesome appearance of having been half skinned. Flush with the four sides of the square was an open concrete trench, approached at intervals by flights of half a dozen stone steps leading to this alley-way.

Malcolm Hay was pushed down one of these, hurried along the alley-way, passing a number of mailed iron doors, and as many barred windows, and was halted before one of the doors whilst the warder who all the time smoked a cigar, produced a key. The door was unlocked, and Hay was thrust in. Malinkoff followed. The door slammed behind them, and they heard the "click-clock" of the steel lock shooting to its socket.

The room was a medium-sized apartment, innocent of furniture save for a table in the centre of the room and a bench which ran round the walls. Light came from a small window giving a restricted view of the courtyard and a barred transom above the doorway. An oblong slit of ground glass behind which was evidently an electric globe served for the night.

There were two occupants of the room, who looked up, one—a grimy, dishevelled priest—blankly, the other with the light of interest in his eyes.

He sat in his shirt-sleeves, his coat being rolled up to serve as a pillow. Above the "bed" hung a Derby hat—an incongruous object. He was short, stout, and fresh coloured, with a startling black moustache elaborately curled at the ends and two grey eyes that were lined around with much laughter. He walked slowly to the party and held out his hand to Malcolm.

"Welcome to the original Bughouse," he said, and from his accent it was impossible to discover whether he was American or English. "On behalf of self an' partner, we welcome you to Bughouse Lodge. When do you go to the chair—he's due to-day," he jerked his thumb at the crooning priest. "I can't say I'm sorry. So far as I am concerned he's been dead ever since they put him here."

Malcolm recognized the little man in a flash. It was his acquaintance of London.

"You don't remember me," smiled Malcolm, "but what is your particular crime?"

The little man's face creased with laughter.

"Shootin' up Tcherekin," he said tersely, and Malinkoff's eyebrows rose.

"You're—Beem—is that how you pronounce it?"

"Bim," said the other, "B-I-M. Christian name Cherry—Cherry Bim; see the idea? Named after the angels. Say, when I was a kid—I've got a photograph way home in Brooklyn to prove it—I had golden hair in long ringlets!"

Malinkoff chuckled softly.

"This is the American who held up Tcherekin and nearly got away with ten million roubles," he said.

Cherry Bim had taken down his Derby and had adjusted it at the angle demanded by the circumstances.

"That's right—but I didn't know they was roubles. I *should* excite my mentality over waste paper! No, we got word that it was French money."

"There was another man in it?" said Malinkoff, lighting a cigarette—there had been no attempt to search them.

"Don't let that match go out!" begged Cherry Bim, and dug a stub from his waistcoat pocket. "Yes," he puffed, "Isaac Moskava—they killed poor old Issy. He was a good feller, but too—too—what's the word when a feller falls to every dame he meets?"

"Impressionable?" suggested Malcolm.

"That's the word," nodded Cherry Bim; "we'd got away with twenty thousand dollars' worth of real sparklers in Petrograd. They used to belong to a princess, and we took 'em off the lady friends of Groobal, the Food Commissioner, and I suggested we should beat it across the Swedish frontier. But no, he had a girl in Moscow—he was that kind of guy who could smell patchouli a million miles away."

Malcolm gazed at the man in wonderment.

"Do I understand that you are a—a——" He hesitated to describe his companion in misfortune, realizing that it was a very delicate position.

"I'm a cavalier of industry," said Cherry Bim, with a flourish.

"Chevalier is the word you want," suggested Malcolm, responding to his geniality.

"It's all one," said the other cheerfully. "It means crook, I guess? Don't think," he said seriously, "don't you think that I'm one of those cheap gun-men you can buy for ten dollars, because I'm not. It was the love of guns that brought me into trouble. It wasn't trouble that brought me to the guns. I could use a gun when I was seven," he said. "My dad—God love him!—lived in Utah, and I was born at Broke Creek and cut my teeth on a '45. I could shoot the tail-feathers off a fly's wing," he said. "I could shoot the nose off a mosquito."

It was the deceased Isaac Moskava who had brought him to Russia, he said. They had been fellow fugitives to Canada, and Isaac, who had friends in a dozen Soviets, had painted an entrancing picture of the pickings which were to be had in Petrograd. They worked their way across Canada and shipped on a Swedish barque, working their passage before the mast. At Stockholm Issy had found a friend, who forwarded them carriage paid to the capital, whereafter things went well.

"Have you got any food?" asked Cherry Bim suddenly. "They starve you here. Did you ever eat *schie*? It's hot water smelling of cabbage."

"Have you been tried?" asked Malinkoff, and the man smiled.

"Tried!" he said contemptuously. "Say, what do you think's goin' to happen to you? Do you think you'll go up before a judge and hire a lawyer to defend you? Not much. If they try you, it's because they've got something funny to tell you. Look here."

He leapt up on to the bench with surprising agility and stood on tiptoe, so that his eyes came level with a little grating in the wall. The opening gave a view of another cell.

"Look," said Cherry Bim, stepping aside, and Malcolm peered through the opening.

At first he could see nothing, for the cell was darker than the room he was in, but presently he distinguished a huddled form lying on the bench, and even as he looked it was galvanized to life. It was an old man who had leaped from the bench mumbling and mouthing in his terror.

"I am awake! I am awake!" he screamed in Russian. "*Gospodar*, observe me! I am awake!"

His wild yells shrunk to a shrill sobbing, and then, with a long sigh, he climbed back to the bench and turned his back to the wall. Malcolm exchanged glances with Malinkoff, who had shared the view.

"What is it?" he asked.

"Come down and I'll tell you. Don't let the old man hear you speak—he's frightened."

"What did he say?" he asked curiously.

Malcolm repeated the words, and Cherry Bim nodded.

"I see. I thought they were stuffing me when they told me, but it's evidently true. He's a Jew," he went on. "Do you think them guys don't kill Jews? Don't you make any mistake about that—they'll kill anybody. This old man has a daughter or a granddaughter, and one of the comrades got fresh with him, so poor old Moses—I don't know his name but he looks like the picture of Moses that we had in our Bible at home—shot at this fellow and broke his jaw, so they sent him to be killed in his sleep."

"In his sleep?" repeated Malcolm incredulously, and Cherry Bim nodded.

"That's it," he said. "So long as he's awake they won't kill him—at least they say so. I guess when his time comes they'll settle him, asleep or awake. The poor old guy thinks that so long as he's awake he's safe—do you get me?"

"It's hellish!" said Malcolm between his teeth. "They must be devils."

"Oh, no, they're not," said Cherry Bim. "I've got nothing on the Soviets. I bet the fellow that invented that way of torturing the old man thinks he's done a grand bit of work. Say, suppose you turned a lot of kids loose to govern the United States, why Broadway would be all cluttered up with dead nursery maids and murdered governesses. That's what's happening in Russia. They don't mean any harm. They're doing all they know to govern, only they don't know much—take no notice of his reverence, he always gets like this round about meal times."

The voice of the black-coated priest grew louder. He stood before the barred window, crossing himself incessantly.

"It is the celebration of the Divine Mystery," said Malinkoff in a low voice, and removed his cap.

"For our holy fathers the high priests Basil the Great, Gregory the Divine, Nicholas of Myra in Lycia, for Peter and Alexis and Jonas, and all holy high priests," groaned the man, "for the holy wonder workers, the disinterested Cosmas and Damiauns, Cyrus and John, Pantaleon and Hermolaus, and all unmercenary saints. . . !

"By the intercession of these, look down upon us, O God!"

He walked back to his seat and, taking compassion upon this man with a white, drawn face, Malcolm went to him.

"Little father," he said, "is there anything we can do for you?"

He produced his cigarette case, but the pope shook his head.

"There is nothing, my son" he replied in a weary voice, which he did not raise above one monotonous tone, "unless you can find the means of bringing Boolba to this cell. Oh, for an hour of the old life!" He raised his hand and his voice at the same moment, and the colour came to his cheeks. "I would take this Boolba," he said, "as holy Ivan took the traitors before the Kremlin, and first I would pour boiling hot water upon him and then ice cold water, and then I would flay him, suspending him by the ankles; then before he was dead I would cut him in four pieces——"

"Phew!" said Malcolm, and walked away.

"Did you expect to find a penitent soul?" asked Malinkoff dryly. "My dear fellow, there is very little difference between the Russian of to-day and the Russian of twelve months ago, with this exception, that the men who had it easy are now having it hard, and those who had to work and to be judged are now the judges."

Malcolm said nothing. He went to the bench and making himself as comfortable as possible he lay down. It was astounding that he could be, as he was, accustomed to captivity in the space of a few hours. He might have lived in bondage all his life, and he would be prepared to live for ever so long as—he did not want to think of the girl, that sweeper of Boolba's.

As to his own fate he was indifferent. Somehow he believed that he was not destined to die in this horrible place, and prayed that at least he might see the girl once more before he fell a victim to the malice of the ex-butler.

To his agony of mind was added a more prosaic distress—he was ravenously hungry, a sensation which was shared by his two companions.

"I've never known them to be so late," complained Cherry Bim regretfully. "There's usually a bit of black bread, if there's nothing else."

He walked to the window and, leaning his arms on the sill, looked disconsolately forth.

"Hi, Ruski!" he yelled at some person unseen, and the other inmates of the room could see him making extravagant pantomime, which produced nothing in the shape of food.

It was three o'clock in the afternoon, and Malcolm was dozing, when they heard the grate of the key in the lock and the slipping of bolts, then the door opened slowly. Malcolm leapt forward.

"Irene—your Highness!" he gasped.

The girl walked into the cell without a word, and put the big basket she had been carrying upon the table. There was a faint colour in the face she turned to Malcolm. Her hands were outstretched to him, and he caught them in his own and held them together.

"Poor little girl!"

She smiled.

"Mr. Hay, you have made good progress in your Russian since I met you last," she said. "General Malinkoff, isn't it?"

The general stood strictly to attention, his hand at his cap—a fact which seemed to afford great amusement to the gaoler who stood in the doorway, and who was an interested spectator.

"It was Boolba's idea that I should bring you food," said the girl, "and I have been ordered to bring it to you every day. I have an idea that he thinks"—she stopped—"that he thinks I like you," she went on frankly, "and of course that is true. I like all people who fly into danger to rescue distressed females," she smiled.

"Can anything be done for you?" asked Malcolm in a low voice. "Can't you get away from this place? Have you no friends?"

She shook her head.

"I have one friend," she said, "who is in even greater danger than I—no, I do not mean you. Mr. Hay"—she lowered her voice—"there may be a chance of getting you out of this horrible place, but it is a very faint chance. Will you promise me that if you get away you will leave Russia at once?"

He shook his head.

"You asked me that once before, your Highness," he said. "I am less inclined to leave Russia now than I was in the old days, when the danger was not so evident."

"Highness"—it was the priest who spoke—"your magnificence has brought me food also? Highness, I served your magnificent father. Do you not remember Gregory the priest in the cathedral at Vladimir?"

She shook her head.

"I have food for you, father," she said, "but I do not recall you."

"Highness" he spoke eagerly and his eyes were blazing, "since you go free, will you not say a prayer for me before the miraculous Virgin?

Or, better still, before the tomb of the holy and sainted Dimitry in the cathedral of the Archangel! And, lady," he seized her hand in entreaty, "before the relics of St. Philip the Martyr in our Holy Cathedral of the Assumption."

Gently the girl disengaged her arm.

"Father, I will pray for you," she said. "Good-bye!" she said to Malcolm, and again extended both her hands, "till to-morrow!"

Malcolm raised the hands to his lips, and stood like a man in a dream, long after the door had slammed behind her.

"Gee!" said the voice of Cherry Bim with a long sigh. "She don't remember me, an' I don't know whether to be glad or sorry—some peach!"

Malcolm turned on him savagely, but it was evident the man had meant no harm.

"She is a friend of mine," he said sharply.

"Sure she is," said the placid Cherry, unpacking the basket, "and the right kind of friend. If this isn't caviare! Say, shut your eyes, and you'd think you were at Rectoris."

Chapter 13

Cherry Bim Makes a Statement

Malcolm was awakened in the night by a scream. He sprang from the bench, his face bathed in perspiration.

"What was that?" he asked hoarsely.

Malinkoff was sitting on the edge of the bench rubbing his eyes.

"I heard something," he yawned.

Only Cheery Bim had not moved. He was lying on his back with his knees up and his hands behind his head, wide awake.

"What was it, Cherry?" asked Malcolm.

Slowly the little man rose and stretched himself.

"I wonder what the time is," he said evasively.

Malcolm looked at his watch.

"Half-past three," he replied.

"He's asleep anyway," said Cherry, nodding towards the recumbent figure of the priest. "He might have been useful—but I forgot the old man's a Jew."

"Do you mean——?" said Malinkoff and glanced at the gate.

Cherry nodded again.

"I never thought they'd carry it out according to programme," he said, "but they did. I heard 'em come in."

There was the thud of a door closing.

"That's the door of his cell. They have taken him out, I guess. The last fellow they killed in there they hung on a hook—just put a rope round his neck and pushed him in a bag. He was a long time dying," he said reflectively, and Malcolm saw that the little man's lower lip was trembling in spite of his calm, matter-of-fact tone.

Malinkoff had walked across to the priest, and had shaken him awake.

"Father," he said, "a man has just died in the next cell. Would you not read the Office of the Dead?"

The priest rose with an ill grace.

"Why should I be awakened from my sleep?" he complained. "Who is this man?"

"I do not know his name," said Malinkoff, "but he is a Jew——"

"A Jew!"

The priest spat on the ground contemptuously.

"What, I speak an office for a Jew?" he demanded, wrath in his face.

"For a man, for a human fellow creature," said Malinkoff sternly, but the priest had gone back to his hard couch, nor would he leave it, and Malinkoff, with a shrug of his shoulders, went back to his bed.

"That is Russia—eternal Russia," he said, and he spoke without bitterness. "Neither Czar nor Soviet will alter it."

They did not go to sleep again. Something was speaking to them from the next cell, something that whimpered and raised its hands in appeal, and they welcomed the daylight, but not the diversion which daylight brought. Again the door banged open, and this time a file of soldiers stood in the entrance.

"Boris Michaelovitch," said the dark figure in the entrance, "it is the hour!"

The priest rose slowly. His face was grey, the hands clasped together before him shook; nevertheless, he walked firmly to the door.

Before the soldiers had closed around him he turned and raised his hand in blessing, and Malinkoff fell upon his knees.

Again the door slammed and the bolts shot home, and they waited in silence.

There was no sound for ten minutes, then came a crash of musketry, so unexpected and so loud that it almost deafened them. A second volley followed, and after an interval a third, and then silence. Cherry Bim wiped his forehead.

"Three this morning," he said unsteadily. "Anyway, it's better than hanging."

There was a long pause, and then:

"Say," he said, "I'm sorry I said I was glad that guy was going."

Malcolm understood.

The day brought Irene at the same hour as on the previous afternoon. She looked around for the priest, and apparently understood, for she made no reference to the missing man.

"If you can get away from here," she said, "go to Preopojenski. That is a village a few versts from here. I tell you this, but——"

She did not complete her sentence, but Malcolm could guess from the hopeless despair in her voice.

"Excuse me, miss," interrupted Cherry Bim. "Ain't there any way of getting a gun for a man? Any old kind of gun," he said urgently; "Colt,

Smith-Wesson, Browning, Mauser—I can handle 'em all—but Colt preferred."

She shook her head sadly.

"It is impossible," she said. "I am searched every time I come in through the lodge."

"In a pie," urged Cherry. "I've read in stories how you can get these things in a pie. Couldn't you make——"

"It's quite impossible," she said. "Even bread is cut into four pieces. That is done in the lodge."

Cherry Bim cast envious eyes on the tall guard at the doorway. He had a long revolver.

"I'll bet," said Cherry bitterly, "he don't know any more about a gun than a school-marm. Why, he couldn't hit a house unless he was inside of it."

"I must go now," said the girl hastily.

"Tell me one thing," said Malcolm. "You spoke yesterday of having one friend. Is that friend Israel Kensky?"

"Hush!" she said.

She took his hand in both of hers.

"Good-bye, Mr. Hay," she said. "I may not come to-morrow."

Her voice was hard and strained, and she seemed anxious to end the interview.

"Boolba told me this morning," she went on, speaking rapidly but little above a whisper, "that he had——certain plans about me. Good-bye, Mr. Hay!"

This time she shook hands with Malinkoff.

"Don't forget the village of Preopojensky," she repeated. "There is only the slightest chance, but if God is merciful and you reach the outside world, you will find the house of Ivan Petroff—please remember that." And in a minute she was gone.

"I wonder what was wrong," said Malcolm. "She was not so frightened when she came in, then she changed as though——"

Looking round he had seen, only for the fraction of a second, a hand through the grating over the bench. Someone had been listening in the next cell, and the girl had seen him. He sprang upon a bench and peered through, in time to see the man vanish beyond the angle of his vision. Malinkoff was lighting his last cigarette.

"My friend," he said, "I have an idea that in the early hours of the morning you and I will go the same way as the unfortunate priest."

"What makes you think so?" asked Malcolm quickly.

"Not only do I, but the Grand Duchess thinks so also," said Malinkoff. "Possibly this is news."

Again the door was opened, and this time it was an officer of the Red Guard who appeared. He had evidently been chosen because of his knowledge of English.

"I want the thief," he said tersely in that language.

"That sounds remarkably like me," said Cherry.

He put on his Derby hat slowly and went forth in his shirt-sleeves. They watched him through the window being taken across the courtyard and through the archway which led to the prison offices and the outer gate.

"They haven't released him, I suppose?" asked Malcolm, and Malinkoff shook his head.

"He is to be interrogated," he said. "Evidently there is something which Boolba wants to know about us, and which he believes this man will tell."

Malcolm was silent, turning matters over in his mind.

"He won't tell anything that will injure us," he said.

"But the man is a crook," said Malinkoff; "that is the word, isn't it?"

"That's the word," agreed Malcolm grimly, "but he's also a man of my own race and breed, and whilst I would not trust him with my pocket-book—or I should not have trusted him before I came in here—I think I can trust him with my life, supposing that he has my life in his hands."

In twenty minutes Cherry Bim was back, very solemn and mysterious until the gaoler was gone. Then he asked:

"Who is Israel Kensky, anyway?"

"Why?" asked Malcolm quickly.

"Because I'm going to make a statement about him—a written statement," he said cheerfully. "I'm going to have a room all to myself," he spoke slowly as though he were repeating something which he had already told himself, "because I am not a quick writer. Then I am going to tell all that she said about Israel Kensky."

"You can tell that in a second," said Malcolm sternly, and the little man raised a lofty hand.

"Don't get up in the air."

"Why have they sent you back now?"

"To ask a question or two," said Cherry.

He put on his coat, examined the interior of his hat thoughtfully, and jammed it down on his head.

"Ten minutes are supposed to elapse," he said melodramatically, "passed in light and airy conversation about a book—the 'Book of—of——'"

"'All-Power'?" said Malcolm.

"That's the fellow. I should say it's the history of this darned place. Here they come."

He pulled down his coat, brushed his sleeves and stepped forward briskly to meet the English-speaking officer.

They passed an anxious two hours before he returned, and, if anything, he was more solemn than ever. He made no reply to their questions, but paced the room, and then he began to sing, and his tune had more reason than rhyme.

"Look through the grating," he chanted, "see if anybody is watching or listening, my honey, oh my honey!"

"There's nobody there," said Malcolm after a brief inspection.

"He'll be back again in five minutes," said Cherry, stopping his song and speaking rapidly. "I told him I wanted to be sure on one point, and he brought me back. I could have done it, but I wouldn't leave you alone."

"Done what?" asked Malcolm.

"Saved myself. Do you know what I saw when I got into that room for the first time? The guy in charge was locking away in a desk three guns and about ten packets of shells. It sounds like a fairy story, but it's true, and it's a desk with a lock that you could open with your teeth!"

It was Malinkoff who saw the possibilities of the situation which the man described.

"And they left you alone in the room?" he asked quickly.

"Sure," said Cherry. "Lift my hat, and lift it steady."

Malcolm pulled his hat up, and the butt of a revolver slipped out.

"There's a Browning there—be careful," said Cherry, ducking his head and pulling off his hat in one motion. "Here's the other under my arm," he put his hand beneath his coat and pulled out a Colt.

"Here are the shells for the automatic. I'll take the long fellow. Now listen, you boys," said Cherry. "Through that gateway at the end of the yard, you come to another yard and another gate, which has a guard on it. Whether we get away or whether we don't, depends on whether our luck is in or out."

"Look!" he whispered, "here comes Percy!"

The door swung open and the officer beckoned Cherry forward with a lift of his chin. Cherry walked toward him and the officer half turned in the attitude of one who was showing another out. Cherry's hand shot out, caught the man by the loose of his tunic and swung him into the room.

"Laugh and the world laughs with you," said Cherry, who had an assortment of literary quotations culled from heaven knows where. "Shout and you sleep alone!"

The muzzle of a long-barrelled '45 was stuck in the man's stomach. He did not see it, but he guessed it, and his hands went up.

"Tie him up—he wears braces," said Cherry. "I'll take that belt of deadly weapons." He pulled one revolver from the man's holster and examined it with an expert's eye. "Not been cleaned for a month," he growled; "you don't deserve to be trusted with a gun."

He strapped the belt about his waist and sighed happily.

They gagged the man with a handkerchief, and threw him ungently upon the bench before they passed through the open door to comparative freedom. Cherry locked and bolted the door behind them, and pulled down the outer shutter, with which, on occasions, the gaoler made life in the cells a little more unendurable by excluding the light. The cells were below the level of the courtyard, and they moved along the trench from which they opened.

Pacing his beat by the gateway was a solitary sentry.

"Stay here," whispered Cherry; "he has seen me going backward and forward, and maybe he thinks I'm one of the official classes."

He mounted the step leading up from the trench, and walked boldly toward the gateway. Nearing the man, he turned to wave a greeting to an imaginary companion. In reality he was looking to see whether there were any observers of the act which was to follow.

Watching him, they did not see exactly what had happened. Suddenly the soldier doubled up like a jack-knife and fell.

Cherry bent over him, lifted the rifle and stood it against the wall, then, exhibiting remarkable strength for so small a man, he picked up the man in his arms and dropped him into the trench which terminated at the gateway. They heard the thud of his body, and, breaking cover, they raced across the yard, joining Cherry, who led the way through the deep arch.

Now they saw the outer barrier. It consisted of a formidable iron grille. To their right was a gloomy building, which Malcolm judged was the bureau of the prison, to the left a high wall. On either side of the gateway was a squat lodge, and before these were half a dozen soldiers, some leaning against the gate, some sitting in the doorway of the lodges, but all carrying rifles.

"This way," said Cherry under his breath, and turned into the office.

The door of the room on his left was open, and into this they walked. It was empty, but scarcely had they closed the door than there were footsteps outside. Cherry, with a gun in each hand, a hard and ugly grin on his fat face, covered the door, but the footsteps passed.

There was a babble of voices outside and a rattle and creak of gates. Malcolm crept to the one window which the office held (he guessed it was here that Cherry had written his "statement"), and peeped cautiously forth.

A big closed auto was entering the gate, and he pulled his head back. Cherry was at his side.

"Somebody visiting—a fellow high up," whispered the latter hoarsely; "they'll come in here, the guy we left in the cell told me he'd want this room. Try that door!"

He pointed to a tall press and Malinkoff was there in a second. The press was evidently used for the storage of stationery. There was one shelf, half way up, laden with packages of paper, and Malinkoff lifted one end. The other slipped and the packets dropped with a crash. But the purring of the auto in the yard was noisy enough to drown the sound unless somebody was outside the door.

"Three can squeeze in—you go first, Mr. Hay."

It was more than a squeeze, it was a torture, but the door closed on them.

Malcolm had an insane desire to laugh, but he checked it at the sound of a voice—for it was the voice of Boolba.

"I cannot stay very long, comrade," he was saying as he entered the room, "but. . ."

The rest was a mumble.

"I will see that she is kept by herself," said a strange voice, evidently of someone in authority at the prison.

Malcolm bit his lips to check the cry that rose.

"Irene!"

". . ." Boolba's deep voice was again a rumble.

"Yes, comrade, I will bring her in. . . let me lead you to a chair."

He evidently went to the door and called, and immediately there was a tramp of feet.

"What does this mean, Boolba?"

Malcolm knew the voice—he had heard it before—and his relief was such that all sense of his own danger passed.

"Sophia Kensky," Boolba was speaking now, "you are under arrest by order of the Soviet."

"Arrest!" the word was screamed, "me——?"

"You are plotting against the Revolution, and your wickedness has been discovered," said Boolba. "*Matinshka!* Little mama, it is ordered!"

"You lie! You lie!" she screeched. "You blind devil—I spit on you! You arrest me because you want the aristocrat Irene Yaroslav! Blind pig!"

"*Prekanzeno, dushinka!* It is ordered, dear little soul," murmured Boolba. "I go back alone—listen! My auto is turning. I go back alone, *drushka*, and who shall be my eyes now that my little mama is gone?"

They heard the chair pushed back as he rose and the scream and flurry as she leapt at him.

"Keep her away, little comrade," roared Boolba. "Keep her away—I am blind; her father blinded me; keep her away!"

It was Cherry Bim who slipped first from the cupboard.

Under the menace of his guns the soldiers fell back.

"Auto Russki—hold up the guard, Hay," he muttered, and Malinkoff jumped through the doorway to the step of the big car in one bound.

Cherry held the room. He spoke no Russian, but his guns were multi-lingual. There was a shot outside before he fired three times into the room. Then he fell back, slamming the door, and jumped into the car as it moved through the open gateway.

Malcolm was on one footboard, Malinkoff by the side of the chauffeur on the other.

So they rocked through the ill-paved streets of Moscow, and rushed the suburban barricade without mishap.

Chapter 14

In the Holy Village

"Preopojensky, but by a circuitous route," said Malinkoff, speaking across the chauffeur. "What about the wires?"

He looked up at the telegraph lines, looping from pole to pole, and Malcolm thrust his head into the window of the limousine to communicate this danger to the sybaritic Mr. Bim, who was spraying himself with perfume from a bottle he had found in the well-equipped interior of the car.

"Stop," said Cherry. "We're well away from Moscow."

At a word from Malinkoff the chauffeur brought the car to a standstill and Cherry slipped out, revolver in hand.

Then to the amazement of Malcolm and the unfeigned admiration of the general, Cherry Bim made good his boast. Four times his gun cracked and at each shot a line broke.

"To be repeated at intervals," said Cherry, climbing into the car. "Wake me in half an hour," and, curling himself up in the luxurious depths of swansdown cushions, he fell asleep.

Happily Malinkoff knew the country to an inch. They were not able to avoid the villages without avoiding the roads, but they circumnavigated the towns. At nightfall they were in the depths of a wood which ran down to the edge of the big lake on which the holy village of Preopojensky stands.

"The chauffeur is not the difficulty I thought he would be," reported Malinkoff; "he used to drive Korniloff in the days when he was a divisional general, and he is willing to throw in his lot with ours."

"Can you trust him!" asked Malcolm.

"I think so," said Malinkoff, "unless we shoot him we simply must trust him—what do you think, Mr. Bim?"

"You can call me Cherry," said that worthy. He was eating bread and sour cheese which had been bought at a fabulous price in one of the villages through which they had passed. Here again they might have been compelled to an act which would have called attention to their lawless character, for they had no money, had it not been for Cherry. He financed the party from the lining of his waistcoat (Malcolm remembered that the little man had never discarded this garment, sleeping or waking) and made a casual reference to the diamonds which had gone to his account via a soi-disant princess and the favourite of a Commissary.

"Anyway," he said, "we could have got it from the chauffeur—he's open to reason."

They did not ask him what argument he would have employed, but were glad subsequently that these arguments had not been used.

What was as necessary as food was petrol. Peter the chauffeur said that there were big army supplies in Preopojensky itself, and undertook to steal sufficient to keep the car running for a week.

They waited until it was dark before they left the cover of the wood, and walked in single file along a cart-track to the half a dozen blinking lights that stood for Preopojensky.

The car they had pulled into deeper cover, marking the place with a splinter of mirror broken from its silver frame.

"Nothing like a mirror," explained Cherry Bim. "You've only to strike a match, and it shows a light for you."

The way was a long one, but presently they came to a good road which crossed the track at right angles, but which curved round until it ran parallel with the path they had followed.

"There is the military store," whispered the chauffeur. "I will go now, my little general."

"I trust you, *drushka*," said Malinkoff.

"By the head of my mother I will not betray you," said the man, and disappeared in the darkness.

After this they held a council of war.

"So far as I can remember, Petroff is the silk merchant," said Malinkoff, "and his house is the first big residence we reach coming from this direction. I remember it because I was on duty at the Coronation of the Emperor, and his Imperial Majesty came to Preopojensky, which is a sacred place for the Royal House. Peter the Great lived here."

Luck was with them, for they had not gone far before they heard a voice bellowing a mournful song, and came up with its owner, a worker in the silk mills (they had long since ceased to work) who was under the influence of methylated spirit—a favourite tipple since vodka had been ukased out of existence.

"Ivan Petroff, son of Ivan?" he hiccoughed.

"Yes, my little dove, it is there. He is a boorjoo and an aristocrat, and there is no Czar and no God!—*prikanzerio*—it is ordered by the Soviet! . . ."

And he began to weep

"No Czar and no God! Long live the Revolution! Evivo! No blessed saints and no Czar! And I was of the Rasholnik! . . ."

They left him weeping by the roadside.

"The Rasholniks are the dissenters of Russia—this village was a hotbed of them, but they've gone the way of the rest," said Malinkoff sadly.

The house they approached was a big wooden structure ornamented with perfectly useless cupolas and domes, so that Malcolm thought at first that this was one of the innumerable churches in which the village abounded.

There was a broad flight of wooden stairs leading to the door, but this they avoided. A handful of gravel at a likely-looking upper window seemed a solution. The response was immediate. Though no light appeared, the window swung open and a voice asked softly:

"Who is that?"

"We are from Irene," answered Malcolm in the same tone.

The window closed, and presently they heard a door unfastened and followed the sound along the path which ran close to the house. It was a small side door that was opened, and Malcolm led the way through.

Their invisible host closed the door behind them, and they heard the clink of a chain.

"If you have not been here before, keep straight on, touching the wall with your right hand. Where it stops turn sharply to the right," said the unknown rapidly.

They followed his directions, and found the branch passage.

"Wait," said the voice.

The man passed them. They heard him turn a handle.

"Straight ahead you will find the door."

They obeyed, and their conductor struck a match and lit an oil lamp. They were in the long room—they guessed that by the glow of the closed stove they had seen as they entered.

The windows were heavily shuttered and curtained, and even the door was hidden under a thick portière. The man who had brought them in was middle-aged and poorly dressed, but then this was a time when everybody in Russia was poorly dressed, and his shabbiness did not preclude the possibility of his being the proprietor of the house, as indeed he was.

He was eyeing them with suspicion, not wholly unjustified, for the patent respectability of Cherry's Derby hat was no compensation for the armoury belted about his rotund middle.

But when the man's eyes fell upon Malinkoff, his whole demeanour changed, and he advanced with outstretched hand.

"General Malinkoff," he said, "you remember me; I entertained you at——"

"At Kieff! Of course!" smiled Malinkoff. "I did not know the Ivan Petroff of Moscow was the Ivan of the Ukraine."

"Now, gentlemen, what is your wish?" asked the man, and Malinkoff explained the object of the visit.

Petroff looked serious.

"Of course, I will do anything her Highness wishes," he said. "I saw her yesterday, and she told me that she had a dear friend in St. Basil." Malcolm tried to look unconcerned under Malinkoff's swift scrutiny and failed. "But I think she wished you to meet another—guest."

He paused.

"He has gone into Moscow to-night against my wishes," he said with trouble in his face; "such an old man——"

"Kensky?" said Malcolm quickly.

"Kensky." The tone was short. "I told him that no good would come of it—her Highness was married to-night."

Malcolm took a step forward, but it was an unsteady step.

"Married?" he repeated. "To whom was she married?"

Petroff looked down at the floor as though he dare not meet the eye of any man and say so monstrous a thing.

"To the servant Boolba," he said.

Chapter 15

The Red Bride

Irene Yaroslav came back to the home which had always been associated in her mind with unhappy memories, to meet the culminating disaster which Fate had wrought. Whatever thoughts of escape she may have treasured in secret were cut into by the sure knowledge that she was watched day and night, and were now finally terminated by the discovery that the big apartment house, a suite of which Boolba had taken for her disposal when he had ousted her from her father's house, was practically in possession of the Soviet Guard.

She drove to the palace with an undisguised escort of mounted men, one on either side of the carriage, one before and one behind, and went up the stairs—those grim stairs which had frightened her as a child and had filled her nights with dreams, passing on her way the now empty bureau which it had been Boolba's whim for her to keep.

Maria Badisikaya, an officer of the Committee for the Suppression of the Counter-Revolution, formerly an operative in the Moscow Cigarette Company, was waiting in the small drawing-room which still retained some of its ancient splendour. Maria was a short, stumpy woman with a slight moustache and a wart on her chin, and was dressed in green satin, cut low to disclose her generous figure. About her stiff, coal-black hair was a heavy diamond bandeau. She was sitting on a settee, her feet hardly touching the ground, cleaning her nails with a little pocket-knife as the girl entered. Evidently this was her maid of honour, and she could have laughed.

The woman glowered up at her and jumped briskly to her feet, closing the knife and slipping it into her corsage.

"You are late, Irene Yaroslav," she said shrilly. "I have something better to do than to sit here waiting for a boorjoo. There is a committee meeting at ten o'clock to-night. How do you imagine I can attend that? Come, come!"

She bustled into an ante-room.

"Here is your dress, my little bride. See, there is everything, even to stockings—Boolba has thought of all, yet he will not see! La! la! What a man!"

Numerous articles of attire were laid out on chairs and on the back of the sofa, and the girl, looking at them, shuddered. It was Boolba's idea—nobody but Boolba would have thought of it. Every garment was of red, blood red, a red which seemed to fill the room with harsh sound. Stockings of finest silk, shoes of russian leather, cobweb underwear—but all of the same hideous hue. In Russia the word "red" is also the word "beautiful." In a language in which so many delicate shades of meaning can be expressed, this word serves a double purpose, doing duty for that which, in the eyes of civilized people, is garish, and that which is almost divine.

Maria's manner changed suddenly. From the impatient, slightly pompous official, conscious of her position, she became obsequious and even affectionate. Possibly she remembered that the girl was to become the wife of the most powerful man in Moscow, whose word was amply sufficient to send even Gregory Prodol to the execution yard, and Gregory's position seemed unassailable.

"I will help you to dress, my little dear," she said. "Let me take your hat, my little dove."

"I would rather be alone," said the girl. "Will you please wait in the next room, Maria Badisikaya?"

"But I can help you so, my little darling," said the woman, fussing about. "A bride has no luck for thirty years if she puts on her own stockings."

"Go!" said the girl imperiously, and the woman cringed.

"Certainly, Excellenz," she stammered, and went out without another word.

The girl changed quickly, and surveyed herself in the pier glass at the end of the room. It was striking but horrible. There came a tap at the door and the agitated Maria entered.

"He has sent for you, my little dove," she said. "Come, take my arm. Do not tremble, my little pretty. Boolba is a good man and the greatest man in Moscow."

She would have taken the girl's arm, but Irene waved her aside, and walked swiftly from the drawing-room into the grand saloon. She wanted the ordeal over as soon as possible.

The room was crowded, and though many of the electric lamps in the great glass chandelier were not in working order and a broken fuse had put half the wall brackets in darkness, the light was almost dazzling. This wonderful saloon, where ten Czars had eaten bread and salt with ten generations of Yaroslavs, was thick with humanity. Some of the men were in uniform, some were in a nondescript costume which was the Soviet compromise between evening-dress and diplomatic uniform. One man wore a correct evening-jacket and a white waistcoat with a perfectly starched shirt, over uniform trousers and top-boots. The women were as weirdly clothed. Some were shabby to the point of rags, a few wore court dresses of the approved pattern, and there was one woman dressed like a man, who smoked all the time. The air was blue with tobacco smoke and buzzing with sound.

As she came into the saloon somebody shouted her name, and there was vigorous applause, not for her, she knew, nor for the name she bore, but for the novelty and the "beauty" of her wedding gown.

At the farther end of the room was a table covered with a red cloth, and behind it sat a man in evening-dress, whom she recognized as one of the newly-appointed magistrates of the city. Nudged behind by Maria, she made her way through the press of people, whose admiring comments were spoken loud enough for her to hear.

"What a little beauty! Too good for a blind man, eh?"

"We have knelt for her many times, now she shall kneel for us."

"Such a dress! This Boolba is a wonderful fellow."

She halted before the table, her hands clasped lightly in front of her. Her head was high, and she met every glance steadily and disdainfully.

The clock struck a quarter after ten when Boolba made his entrance amidst a storm of applause.

They had never seen him in such a uniform before. Some thought it was a new costume which had been sanctioned by the supreme Soviet for its Commissaries; others that it had been planned especially for the marriage. Irene alone knew it, and a cold, disdainful smile lit for a moment her expressionless face.

She had seen Boolba in knee-breeches and white silk stockings before; she knew the coat of green and gold which the retainers of the house of Yaroslav wore on state occasions. Boolba was marrying her in his butler's livery—a delicate piece of vengeance.

The ceremony was short, and, to the girl, unreal. Religious marriages, though they had not altogether been banned, were regarded by the official Russia as unnecessary, and a new marriage service had been designed, which confined the ceremony to the space of a few minutes. The attempts to abolish marriage altogether had been strenuously opposed, not so much by the public women who were on the innumerable councils and committees, but by the wives of the more important members of the organization.

Boolba was led to her side, and reached out his hand gropingly, and in very pity of his blindness she took it. Questions were asked him, to which he responded and similar questions were asked her, to which she made no reply. The whole ceremony was a farce, and she had agreed to it only because it gave her a little extra time, and every minute counted. From the moment the magistrate pronounced the formula which made them, in the eyes of the Soviet law at any rate, man and wife, Boolba never loosened his hold of her.

He held her hand in his own big, hot palm, until it was wet and her fingers lost all feeling. From group to group they moved, and when they crossed the dancing space of the saloon, the revellers stepped aside to allow the man to pass. She noticed that in the main they confined themselves to country dances, some of which were new to her. And all the time Boolba kept up a continuous conversation in an undertone, pinching her hand gently whenever he wanted to attract her attention.

"Tell me, my new eyes, my little pigeon of God, what are they doing now? Do you see Mishka Gurki? She is a silly woman. Tell me, my little pet, if you see her. Watch her well, and tell me how she looks at me. That woman is an enemy of the Revolution and a friend of Sophia Kensky. . . Ah! it is sad about your poor friends."

The girl turned cold and clenched her teeth to take the news which was coming.

"They tried to escape and they were shot down by our brave guard. I would have pardoned them for your sake, all but the thief, who broke the jaw of comrade Alex Alexandroff. Yes, I would have pardoned them to-night, because I am happy. Else they would have died with Sophia Kensky in the morning. . . Do I not please you, that I put away this woman, who was my eyes and saw for me—all for your sake, my little pigeon, all for your sake! . . . Do you see a big man with one eye? He has half my misfortune, yet he sees a million times more than Boolba! That is the butcher Kreml—some day he shall see the Kreml*," he chuckled. . . "Why do you not speak, my darling little mama? Are you thinking of the days when I was Boolba the slave? Na, na, *stoi*! Think of to-day, to-night, my little child of Jesus!"

---

* "Kreml" is literally Kremlin, one of the places of detention in Moscow.

There were times when she could have screamed, moments of madness when she longed to pick up one of the champagne bottles which littered the floor, and at intervals were thrown with a crash into a corner of the room, and strike him across that great brutal face. There were times when she was physically sick and the room spun round and round and she would have fallen but for the man's arm. But the hour she dreaded most of all came at last, when, one by one, with coarse jests at her expense, the motley company melted away and left her alone with the man.

"They have all gone?" he asked eagerly. "Every one?"

He clutched more tightly.

"To my room. We have a supper for ourselves. They are pigs, all these fellows, my little beautiful."

The old carpet was still on the stairs, she noticed dully. Up above used to be her own room, at the far end of the long passage. She had a piano there once. She wondered whether it was still there. There used to be a servant at the head and at the foot of these stairs—a long, green-coated Cossack, to pass whom without authority was to court death. The room on the left had been her father's—two big saloons, separated by heavy silken curtains; his bureau was at one end, his bedroom at the other.

It was into the bureau that the man groped his way. A table had been set, crowded with bottles and glasses, piled with fruit, sweetmeats, and at the end the inevitable samovar.

"I will lock the door," said Boolba. "Now you shall kiss me on the eyes and on the mouth and on the cheeks, making the holy cross."

She braced herself for the effort, and wrenched free. In a flash he came at her, and his hands caught the silken gown at the shoulder. She twisted under his arm, leaving a length of tattered and torn silk in his hand, and the marks of his finger-nails upon her white shoulder. He stopped and laughed—a low, gurgling laugh—and it was to the girl like the roar of some subterranean river heard from afar.

"Oh, Highness," he mocked, "would you rob a blind man of his bride? Then let us be blind together!"

He blundered to the door. There was a click, and the room was in darkness.

"I am better than you now," he said. "I hear you in the dark; I can almost see you. You are by the corner of the table. Now you are pushing a chair. Little pigeon, come to me!"

Whilst he was talking she was safe because she could locate him. It was when he was silent that she was filled with wild fear. He moved as softly as a cat, and it seemed that his boast of seeing in the dark was almost justified. Once his hand brushed her and she shrank back only just in time. The man was breathing heavily now, and the old, mocking terms of endearment had changed.

"Come to me, Irene Yaroslav!" he roared. "Have I not often run to you? Have I not waited throughout the night to take your wraps and bring you coffee? Now you shall wait on me by Inokente! You shall be eyes and hands for me, and when I am tired of you, you shall go the way of Sophia Kensky."

She was edging her way to the door. Once she could switch on the light she was safe, at any rate for the time being. There was a long silence, and, try as she did, she could not locate him. He must have been crouching near the door, anticipating her move, for as her hand fell on the switch and the lights sprang into being, he leapt at her. She saw him, but too late to avoid his whirling hands. In a second he had her in his arms. The man was half mad. He cursed and blessed her alternately, called her his little pigeon and his little devil in the same breath. She felt the tickle of his beard against her bare shoulder, and strove to push him off.

"Come, my little peach," he said. "Who shall say that there is no justice in Russia, when Yaroslav's daughter is the bride of Boolba!"

His back was to the curtain, and he was half lifting, half drawing her to the two grey strips which marked its division, when the girl screamed.

"Again, again, my little dear," grinned Boolba. "That is fine music."

But it was not her own danger which had provoked the cry. It was that vision, twice seen in her lifetime, of dead white hands, blue-veined, coming from the curtain and holding this time a scarlet cord.

It was about Boolba's neck before he realized what had happened. With a strangled cry he released the girl, and she fell back again on the table, overturning it with a crash.

"This way, Highness," said a hollow voice, and she darted through the curtains.

She heard the shock of Boolba's body as it fell to the ground, and then Israel Kensky darted past her, flung open the door and pushed her through.

"The servants' way," he said, and she ran to the narrow staircase which led below to the kitchen, and above to the attics in which the servants slept.

Down the stairs, two at a time, she raced, the old man behind her. The stairway ended in a square hall. There was a door, half ajar, leading to the kitchen, which was filled with merrymakers, and a second door leading into the street, and this was also open. She knew the way blindfolded. They were in what had been the coach-yard of the Palace, and she knew there were half a dozen ways into the street. Israel chose the most unlikely, one which led again to the front of the house.

A drosky was waiting, and into this he bundled her, jumping in by her side, holding her about the waist as the driver whipped up his two horses and sped through the deserted streets of Moscow.

Chapter 16

THE BOOK OF ALL-POWER

Malcolm was the first to hear the sound of wheels on the roadway, and the party listened in silence till a low whistle sounded and their host darted out of the room.

"What was that?" asked Malinkoff. "Somebody has come to the front door."

A few minutes later Petroff staggered through the doorway, carrying the limp figure of Irene. It was Malcolm who took the girl in his arms and laid her upon the sofa.

"She is not dead," said a voice behind him.

He looked up; it was Israel Kensky. The old man looked white and ill. He took the glass of wine which Ivan brought him with a shaking hand, and wiped his beard as he looked down at the girl. There was neither friendliness nor pity in his glance, only the curious tranquillity which comes to the face of a man who has done that which he set out to do.

"What of Boolba?" asked Petroff eagerly

"I think he lives," said Kensky, and shook his head. "I am too weak and too old a man to have killed him. I put the cord about his neck and twisted it with a stick. If he can loosen the cord he will live; if he cannot, he will die. But I think he was too strong a man to die."

"Did he know it was you?" asked Petroff.

Kensky shook his head.

"What is the hour?" he asked, and they told him that it was two o'clock.

"Sophia Kensky dies at four," he said, in such a tone of unconcern that even Malinkoff stared at him.

"It is right that she should die," said Kensky, and they marvelled that he, who had risked his life to save one of the class which had persecuted his people for hundreds of years, should speak in so matter-of-fact tones about the fate of his own blood. "She betrayed her race and her father. It is the old law of Israel, and it is a good law. I am going to sleep."

"Is there a chance that you have been followed?" asked Malinkoff, and Kensky pulled at his beard thoughtfully.

"I passed a watchman at the barricade, and he was awake—that is the only danger."

He beckoned to Malcolm, and, loth as the young man was to leave the girl's side, now that she was showing some signs of recovering consciousness, he accompanied the old man from the room.

"*Gospodar*," said Israel Kensky (it sounded strange to hear that old title), "once you carried a book for me."

"I remember." Malcolm smiled in spite of himself.

"'The Book of All-Power,'" repeated the Jew quietly. "It is in my room, and I shall ask you to repeat your service. That book I would give to the Grand Duchess, for I have neither kith nor child, and she has been kind to me."

"But surely, Kensky," protested Malcolm, "you, as an intelligent man, do not believe in the potency of books or charms of incantations?"

"I believe in the 'Book of All-Power,'" said Kensky calmly. "Remember, it is to become the property of the Grand Duchess Irene. I do not think I have long to live," he added. "How my death will come I cannot tell, but it is not far off. Will you go with me now and take the book?"

Malcolm hesitated. He wanted to get back to the girl, but it would have been an ungracious act not to humour the old man, who had risked so much for the woman he loved. He climbed the stairs to the little bedroom, and waited at the door whilst Kensky went in. Presently the old man returned; the book was now stitched in a canvas wrapping, and Malcolm slipped the book into his pocket. The very act recalled another scene which had been acted a thousand miles away, and, it seemed, a million years ago.

"Now let us go down," said Kensky.

"Lord," he asked, as Malcolm's foot was on the stair, "do you love this young woman?"

It would have been the sheerest affectation on his part to have evaded the question.

"Yes, Israel Kensky," he replied, "I love her," and the old man bowed his head.

"You are two Gentiles, and there is less difference in rank than in race," he said. "I think you will be happy. May the Gods of Jacob and of Abraham and of David rest upon you and prosper you. Amen!"

Never had benediction been pronounced upon him that felt so real, or that brought such surprising comfort to the soul of Malcolm Hay. He felt as if, in that dingy stairway, he had received the very guerdon of manhood, and he went downstairs spiritually strengthened, and every doubt in his mind set at rest.

The girl half rose from the couch as he came to her, and in her queer, impulsive way put out both her hands. Five minutes before he might have hesitated; he might have been content to feel the warmth of her palms upon his. But now he knelt down by her side, and, slipping one arm about her, drew her head to his shoulder. He heard the long-drawn sigh of happiness, he felt her arm creep about his neck, and he forgot the world and all the evil and menace it held: he forgot the grave Malinkoff, the interested Cherry Bim, still wearing his Derby hat on the back of his head, and girt about with the weapons of his profession. He forgot everything except that the world was worth living for. There lay in his arms a fragrant and a beautiful thing.

It was Petroff who put an end to the little scene.

"I have sent food into the wood for you," he said, "and my man has come back to tell me that your chauffeur is waiting by the car. He has all the petrol that he requires, and I do not think you should delay too long."

The girl struggled to a sitting position, and looked with dismay at her scarlet bridal dress.

"I cannot go like this," she said.

"I have your trunk in the house, Highness," said Petroff, and the girl jumped up with a little cry of joy.

"I had forgotten that," she said.

She had forgotten also that she was still weak, for she swayed and would have stumbled, had not Malcolm caught her.

"Go quickly, Highness," said Petroff urgently. "I do not think it would be safe to stay here—safe for you or for Kensky. I have sent one of my men on a bicycle to watch the Moscow road."

"Is that necessary?" asked Malinkoff. "Are you suspect?"

Petroff nodded.

"If Boolba learns that Kensky passed this way, he will guess that it is to me that he came. I was in the service of the Grand Duke, and if it were not for the fact that a former workman of mine is now Assistant Minister of Justice in Petrograd, I should have been arrested long ago. If Boolba finds Israel Kensky here, or the Grand Duchess, nothing can save me. My only hope is to get you away before there is a search. Understand, little general," he said earnestly, "if you had not the car, I would take all risks and let you stay until you were found."

"That seems unnecessary," said Malinkoff. "I quite agree. What do you say, Kensky?"

The old man, who had followed Malcolm down the stairs, nodded.

"I should have shot Boolba," he said thoughtfully, "but it would have made too much noise."

"You should have used the knife, little father," said Petroff, but Kensky shook his head.

"He wears chain armour under his clothes," he said. "All the commissaries do."

Preparations for the journey were hurriedly made. The girl's trunk had proved a veritable storehouse, and she came down in a short tweed skirt and coat, her glorious hair hidden under a black tam o' shanter, and Malcolm could scarcely take his eyes from her.

"You have a coat," said the practical Malinkoff. "That is good—you may need it."

Crash!

It was the sound of a rifle butt against the door which struck them dumb. Muffled by the thick wood, the voice of the knocker yet came clearly: "Open in the name of the Revolution!"

Petroff blinked twice, and on his face was a look as though he could not believe his ears. The girl shrank to Malcolm's side, and Malinkoff stroked his beard softly. Only Cherry Bim seemed to realize the necessities of the moment, and he pulled both guns simultaneously and laid them noiselessly on the table before him.

"Open in the name of the Revolution!"

A hiss from Kensky brought them round. He beckoned them through the door by which they had made their original entry to the room, and pointed to the light. He gripped Petroff by the shoulder.

"Upstairs to your bedroom, friend," he said. "Put on your night-shirt and talk to them through the window."

Down the two passages they passed and came to the little door, which Kensky unchained and opened. He put his lips close to Malinkoff's ears.

"Do you remember the way you came?" he asked, and the general nodded and led the way.

Last but one came Cherry Bim, a '45 in each hand. There were no soldiers in view at the back of the house, but Malinkoff could hear their feet on some unknown outside road, and realized that the house was in process of being surrounded, and had the man who knocked at the door waited until this encirclement had been completed, there would have been no chance of escape.

They struck the main road, and found the cart track leading to the wood, and none challenged them. There was no sound from the house, and apparently their flight had not been discovered.

Kensky brought up the rear in spite of Cherry's frenzied injunctions, delivered in the four words of Russian which he knew, to get a move on. They had reached the fringe of the wood when the challenge came. Out of the shadow rode a horseman, and brought his charger across the path.

"Halt!" he cried.

The party halted, all except Cherry, who stepped from the path and moved swiftly forward, crouching low, to give the sentry no background.

"Who is that?" asked the man on the horse. "Speak, or I'll fire!"

He had unslung his carbine, and they heard the click of the bolt as the breech opened and closed.

"We are friends, little father," said Malinkoff.

"Give me your names," said the sentry, and Malinkoff recited with glib ease a list of Russian patronymics.

"That is a lie," said the man calmly. "You are boorjoos—I can tell by your voices," and without further warning he fired into the thick of them.

The second shot which came from the night followed so quickly upon the first that for the second time in like circumstances the girl thought only one had been fired. But the soldier on the horse swayed and slid to the earth before she knew what had happened.

"Go right ahead," said the voice of Cherry Bim.

He had caught the bridle of the frightened horse, and had drawn him aside. They quickened their steps and came up to the car, which the thoughtful chauffeur had already cranked up at the sound of the shots.

"Where is Kensky?" asked Malcolm suddenly, "did you see him, Cherry?"

A pause.

"Why, no," said Cherry, "I didn't see him after the lamented tragedy."

"We can't leave the old man," said Malcolm.

"Wait," said the little gun-man. "I will go back and look for him."

Five minutes, ten passed and still there was no sign or sound of Israel Kensky or of Cherry. Then a shot broke the stillness of the night, and another and another.

"Two rifles and one revolver," said Malinkoff. "Get into the car, Highness. Are you ready, Peter?"

There was another shot and then a fusillade. Then came slow footsteps along the cart track, and the sound of a man's windy breathing.

"Take him, somebody," said Cherry.

Malinkoff lifted the inanimate figure from Cherry's shoulder and carried him into the car. A voice from the darkness shouted a command, there was a flash of fire and the "zip" of a bullet.

"Let her go, Percy," said Cherry, and blazed away with both guns into the darkness.

He leapt for the footboard and made it by a miracle, and only once did they hear him cry as if in pain.

"Are you hit?" asked Malcolm anxiously.

"Naw!" drawled his voice jerkily, for the road hereabouts was full of holes, and even speech was as impossible as even riding. "Naw," he said. "I nearly lost my hat."

He spoke only once again that night, except to refuse the offer to ride inside the car. He preferred the footboard, he said, and explained that as a youth it had been his ambition to be a fireman.

"I wonder," he said suddenly, breaking the silence of nearly an hour.

"What do you wonder?" asked Malinkoff, who sat nearest to the window, where Cherry stood.

"I wonder what happened to that boy on the bicycle?"

Chapter 17

On the Road

Israel Kensky died at five o'clock in the morning. They had made a rough attempt to dress the wound in his shoulder, but, had they been the most skilful of surgeons with the best appliances which modern surgery had invented at their hands, they could not have saved his life. He died literally in the arms of Irene, and they buried him in a little forest on the edge of a sluggish stream, and Cherry Bim unconsciously delivered the funeral oration.

"This poor old guy was a good fellow," he said. "I ain't got nothing on the Jews as a class, except their habit of prosperity, and that just gets the goat of people like me, who hate working for a living. He was straight and white, and that's all you can expect any man to be, or any woman either, with due respect to you, miss. If any of you gents would care to utter a few words of prayer, you'll get a patient hearing from me, because I am naturally a broad-minded man."

It was the girl who knelt by the grave, the tears streaming down her cheeks, but what she said none heard. Cherry Bim, holding his hat crown outward across his breast, produced the kind of face which he thought adequate to the occasion; and, after the party had left the spot, he stayed behind. He rejoined them after a few minutes, and he was putting away his pocket-knife as he ran.

"Sorry to keep you, ladies and gents," he said, "but I am a sentimental man in certain matters. I always have been and always shall be."

"What were you doing?" asked Malcolm, as the car bumped along.

Cherry Bim cleared his throat and seemed embarrassed.

"Well, to tell you the truth," he said. "I made a little cross and stuck it over his head."

"But——" began Malcolm, and the girl's hand closed his mouth.

"Thank you, Mr. Bim," she said. "It was very, very kind of you."

"Nothing wrong, I hope?" asked Cherry in alarm.

"Nothing wrong at all," said the girl gently.

That cross over the grave of the Jew was to give them a day's respite. Israel Kensky had left behind him in the place where he fell a fur hat bearing his name. From the quantity of blood which the pursuers found, they knew that he must have been mortally wounded, and it was for a grave by the wayside that the pursuing party searched and found. It was the cross at his head which deceived them and led them to take the ford and try along the main road to the south of the river, on the banks of which Kensky slept his last dreamless sleep.

The danger for the fugitives was evident.

"The most we can hope," said Malinkoff, "is to escape detection for two days, after which we must abandon the car."

"Which way do you suggest?" asked Malcolm.

"Poland or the Ukraine," replied the general quickly. "The law of the Moscow Soviet does not run in Little Russia or in Poland. We may get to Odessa, but obviously we cannot go much farther like this. I have—or had," he corrected himself, "an estate about seventy versts from here, and I think I can still depend upon some of my people—if there are any left alive. The car we must get rid of, but that, I think, will be a simple matter."

They were now crossing a wide plain, which reminded Malcolm irresistibly of the steppes of the Ukraine, and apparently had recalled the same scene to Irene and Malinkoff. There was the same sweep of grass-land, the same riot of flowers; genista, cornflour and clover dabbled the green, and dwarf oaks and poverty-stricken birches stood in lonely patches.

"Here is a Russia which the plough has never touched," said Malinkoff. "Does it not seem to you amazing that the Americans and British who go forth to seek new colonies, should lure our simple people to foreign countries, where the mode of living, the atmosphere, is altogether different from this, when here at their doors is a new land undiscovered and unexploited?"

He broke off his homily to look out of the window of the car. He had done that at least a dozen times in the past half-hour.

"We're going fairly fast," said Malcolm. "You do not think anything will overtake us?"

"On the road—no," said Malinkoff, "but I am rather nervous crossing this plain, where there is practically no cover at all, and the car is raising clouds of dust."

"Nervous of what?"

"Aeroplanes," said Malinkoff. "Look, there is a pleasant little wood. I suggest that we get under cover until night falls. The next village is Truboisk, which is a large market centre and is certain to hold local officers of the Moscow Soviet."

Both his apprehensions and his judgment were justified, for scarcely had the car crept into the cover of green boughs, than a big aeroplane was sighted. It was following the road and at hardly a hundred feet above them. It passed with a roar. They watched it until it was a speck in the sky.

"They are taking a lot of trouble for a very little thing. Russia must be law-abiding if they turn their aeroplanes loose on a party of fugitive criminals!"

"Boolba has told his story," said Malinkoff significantly. "By this time you are not only enemies of the Revolution, but you are accredited agents of capitalistic Governments. You have been sent here by your President to stir up the bourgeois to cast down the Government, because of British investments. Mr. Bim will be described as a secret service agent who has been employed to assassinate either Trotsky or Lenin. If you could only tap the official wireless," said Malinkoff, "you would learn that a serious counter-revolutionary plot has been discovered, and that American financiers are deeply involved. Unless, of course," corrected Malinkoff, "America happens to be in favour in Petrograd, in which case it will be English financiers."

Malcolm laughed.

"Then we are an international incident?" he said.

"You are an 'international incident,'" agreed Malinkoff gravely.

Cherry Bim, sitting on the step, smoking a long cigar, a box of which Petroff had given him as a parting present—looked up, blowing out a blue cloud.

"A secret service agent?" he said. "That's a sort of fly cop, isn't it?"

"That's about it, Cherry," replied Malcolm.

"And do you think they'll call me a fly cop?" said the interested Cherry.

Malinkoff nodded, and the gun-man chewed on his cigar.

"Time brings its revenges, don't it?" he said. "Never, oh never, did I think that I should be took for a fellow from the Central Office! It only shows you that if a guy continues on the broad path that leadeth to destruction, and only goes enough, he'll find Mrs. Nemesis—I think that's the name of the dame."

Malinkoff strolled to the edge of the wood and came back hurriedly.

"The aeroplane is returning," he said, "and is accompanied by another."

This time neither machine took the direct route. They were sweeping the country methodically from side to side, and Malinkoff particularly noticed that they circled about a smaller wood two miles away and seemed loth to leave it.

"What colour is the top of this car?" he asked, and Bim climbed up.

"White," he said. "Is there time to put on a little of this 'camelflage' I've heard so much about?"

The party set to work in haste to tear down small branches of trees and scraps of bushes, and heap them on to the top of the car. Cherry Bim, who had the instinct of deception, superintending the actual masking of the roof, and as the sun was now setting detected a new danger.

"Let all the windows down," said Cherry. "Put a coat over the glass screen and sit on anything that shines."

They heard the roar of the aeroplane coming nearer and crouched against the trunk of a tree. Suddenly there was a deafening explosion which stunned the girl and threw her against Malcolm. She half-rose to run but he pulled her down.

"What was it?" she whispered.

"A small bomb," said Malcolm. "It is an old trick of airmen when they are searching woods for concealed bodies of infantry. Somebody is bound to run out and give the others away."

Cherry Bim, fondling his long Colt, was looking glumly at the cloud of smoke which was billowing forth from the place where the bomb had dropped. Round and round circled the aeroplane, but presently, as if satisfied with its scrutiny, it made off, and the drone of the engine grew fainter and fainter.

"War's hell," said Cherry, wiping his pallid face with a hand that shook.

"I can't quite understand it," said Malinkoff. "Even supposing that Boolba has told his story, there seems to be a special reason for this urgent search. They would, of course, have communicated——"

He fell silent.

"Has Boolba any special reasons, other than those we know?" he asked.

Malcolm remembered the "Book of All-Power" and nodded.

"Have you something of Kensky's?" asked Malinkoff quickly. "Not that infernal book?"

He looked so anxious that Malcolm laughed.

"Yes, I have that infernal book. As a matter of fact, it is the infernal book of the Grand Duchess now."

"Mine?" she said in surprise.

"Kensky's last words to me were that this book should become your property," said Malcolm, and she shivered.

"All my life seems to have been associated with the search for that dreadful book," she said. "I wonder if it is one of Kensky's own binding. You know," she went on, "that Israel Kensky bound books for a hobby? He bound six for me, and they were most beautifully decorated."

"He was a rich man, was he not?" asked Malcolm.

She shook her head.

"He was penniless when he died," she said quietly. "Every store of his was confiscated and his money was seized by order of the new Government. I once asked him definitely why he did not turn to his 'Book of All-Power' for help. He told me the time had not yet come."

"May I see the book?"

Malcolm took the volume with its canvas cover from his pocket, and the girl looked at it seriously.

"Do you know, I have half a mind to throw it into the fire?" she said, pointing to the smouldering wood where the bomb had fallen. "There seems something sinister, something ominous about its possession that fills me with terror."

She looked at it for a moment musingly, then handed it back to Malcolm.

"Poor Israel!" she said softly, "and poor Russia!"

They waited until darkness fell before they moved on. Malinkoff had an idea that there was a crossroad before the town was reached, and progress was slow in consequence, because he was afraid of passing it. He was determined now not to go through the village, which lay directly ahead. The fact that the aeroplane had been able to procure a recruit, pointed to the existence of a camp of considerable dimensions in the neighbourhood and he was anxious to keep away from armed authority.

It was a tense hour they spent—tense for all except Cherry Bim, who had improvised a cushion on the baggage carrier at the back of the car, and had affixed himself so that he could doze without falling off. The side road did not appear, and Malinkoff grew more and more apprehensive. There were no lights ahead, as there should be if he were approaching the village. Once he thought he saw dark figures crouching close to the ground as the car passed, but put this down to nerves. Five hundred yards beyond, he discovered that his eyes had not deceived him. A red light appeared in the centre of the road, and against the skyline—for they were ascending a little incline at the moment—a number of dark figures sprang into view.

The chauffeur brought the car to a halt with a jerk, only just in time, for his lamps jarred against the pole which had been placed across the road.

Malcolm had drawn his revolver, but the odds were too heavy, besides which, in bringing his car to a standstill, the driver had shut off his engine and the last hope of bunking through had disappeared.

A man carrying a red lamp came to the side of the car, and flashed the light of a torch over the occupants.

"One, two, three, four," he counted. "There should be five."

He peered at them separately.

"This is the aristocrat general, this is the American revolutionary, this is the woman. There is also a criminal. Did any man jump out?" he asked somebody in the darkness, and there was a chorus of "No!"

Footsteps were coming along the road; the guard which had been waiting to close them in from the rear, was now coming up. The man with the lamp, who appeared to be an officer, made a circuit of the car and discovered the carrier seat, but its occupant had vanished.

"There was a man here, you fools," he shouted. "Search the road; he cannot have gone far. Look!"

He put the light on the road.

"There are his boots. You will find him amongst the bushes. Search quickly."

Malcolm, at the girl's side, put his arm about her shoulder.

"You are not afraid?" he said gently, and she shook her head.

"I do not think I shall ever be afraid again," she replied. "I have faith in God, my dear. Cherry has escaped?" she asked.

"I think so," he replied in a guarded tone. "He must have seen the soldiers and jumped. They have just found his boots in the roadway."

The officer came back at that moment.

"You have weapons," he said. "Give them to me."

It would have been madness to disobey the order, and Malcolm handed over his revolver and Malinkoff followed suit. Not satisfied with this, the man turned them out in the road whilst he conducted a search.

"Get back," he said after this was over. "You must go before the Commissary for judgment. The woman is required in Moscow, but we shall deal summarily with the foreigner and Malinkoff, also the little thief, when we find him."

He addressed the chauffeur.

"I shall sit by your side, and if you do not carry out my instructions I shall shoot you through the head, little pigeon," he said. "Get down and start your machine."

Chapter 18

THE MONASTERY OF
ST. BASIL THE LEPER

He gave an order to the soldiers, and the barrier was removed, then he struck a match and lit a flare which burnt a dazzling red flame for half a minute.

"A signal," said Malinkoff, "probably to notify our capture."

A few minutes later, with a soldier on either footboard, and the officer sitting beside the chauffeur, the car sped through the night, checking only before it came to the cross-roads which Malinkoff had sought for. Turning to the left, the car swung into a road narrower and less comfortable for the passengers.

"I wonder if they will catch our brave friend," said the girl.

"They will be sorry if they do," replied Malcolm dryly. "Cherry will not be caught as we were."

Ahead of them and to the right apparently, on a hill by their height, a dozen fires were burning, and Malinkoff judged that the camp they were approaching was one of considerable size. He guessed it was a concentration camp where the Reds were preparing for their periodical offensive against the Ukraine. It must be somewhere in this district that the Polish Commissioners were negotiating with the Supreme Government—an event which had set Moscow agog.

An eerie experience this, riding through the dark, the figures of the soldier guards on either footboard gripping to the posts of the car. Bump, bump, bump it went, swaying and jolting, and then one of the guards fell off. They expected him to jump on the footboard again, for the auto was going at a slow pace, but to their surprise he did not reappear. Then a similar accident happened to the man on the other footboard. He suddenly let go his hold and fell backwards.

"What on earth——" said Malcolm.

"Look, look!" whispered the girl.

A foot and a leg had appeared opposite the window, and it came from the roof of the car. Then another foot, and the bulk of a body against the night.

"It's Cherry!" whispered the girl.

Swiftly he passed the window and came to the side of the officer, whose head was turned to the chauffeur.

"Russki," said Cherry, "*stoi*!"

"Stop!" was one of the four Russian words he knew, and the chauffeur obeyed, just at the moment when the car came to where the road split into two, one running to the right and apparently to the camp, the other and the older road dipping down to a misty valley.

The Red officer saw the gun under his nose and took intelligent action. His two hands went up and his revolver fell with a clatter at the chauffeur's feet. Deftly Cherry relieved him of the remainder of his arms.

By this time Malcolm was out of the car, and a brief council of war was held.

To leave the man there would be to ask for trouble. To shoot him was repugnant even to Cherry, who had constituted himself the official assassin of the party.

"We shall have to take him along," said Malinkoff. "There are plenty of places where we can leave him in the night, and so long as he does not know which way we go, I do not think he can do us any harm."

The Red officer took his misfortune with the philosophy which the chauffeur had displayed in similar circumstances.

"I have no malice, little general," he said. "I carry out my orders as a soldier should. For my part I would as soon cry 'Long live the Czar!' as 'Long live the Revolution!' If you are leaving Russia I shall be glad to go with you, and I may be of service because I know all the latest plans for arresting you. There is a barrier on every road, even on this which you are taking now, unless," he added thoughtfully, "it is removed for the Commissary Boolba."

"Is he coming this way?" asked Malcolm.

"You saw me fire a flare," said the man. "That was a signal to the camp that you were captured. The news will be telegraphed to Moscow, and Boolba will come to sentence the men and take back his wife."

He evidently spoke in the terms of his instructions.

"What road will he take, little soldier?" asked Malinkoff.

"The Tver road," said the man. "It is the direct road from Moscow, and we shall cross it very quickly. At the crossing are four soldiers and an under officer, but no barricade. If you will direct me I will tell them a lie and say that we go to meet Boolba."

"We're in his hands to some extent," said Malinkoff, "and my advice is that we accept his offer. He is not likely to betray us."

The car resumed its journey, and Cherry, who had taken his place inside, explained the miracle which had happened.

"I saw the first lot of soldiers we passed," he said, "and when the car stopped suddenly I knew what had happened. I took off my boots and climbed on to the roof. I only made it just in time. The rest was like eating pie."

"You didn't shoot the soldiers who were standing on the footboard, did you?" asked Malcolm. "I heard no shots."

Cherry shook his head.

"Why shoot 'em?" he said. "I had only to lean over and hit 'em on the bean with the butt end of my gun, and it was a case of 'Where am I, nurse?'"

Half an hour's drive brought them to the cross-roads, and the four apathetic sentries who, at the word of the Red officer, stood aside to allow the car to pass. They were now doubling back on their tracks, running parallel with the railroad (according to Malinkoff) which, if the officer's surmise was accurate, was the one on which Boolba was rushing by train to meet them. So far their auto had given them no trouble, but twenty miles from the camp both the front tyres punctured simultaneously. This might have been unimportant, for they carried two spare wheels, only it was discovered that one of these was also punctured and had evidently been taken out of use the day on which they secured the car. There was nothing to do but to push the machine into a field, darken the windows and allow the chauffeur to make his repairs on the least damaged of the tubes. They shut him into the interior of the car with the Red officer who volunteered his help, furnished him with a lamp, and walked down the road in the faint hope of discovering some cottage or farm where they could replenish their meagre store of food.

Half an hour's walking brought them to a straggling building which they approached with caution.

"It is too large for a farm," said Malinkoff; "it is probably one of those monasteries which exist in such numbers in the Moscow Government."

The place was in darkness and it was a long time before they found the entrance, which proved to be through a small chapel, sited in one corner of the walled enclosure. The windows of the chapel were high up, but Malcolm thought he detected a faint glow of light in the interior, and it was this flicker which guided them to the chapel. The door was half open, and Malinkoff walked boldly in. The building, though small, was beautiful. Green malachite columns held up the groined roof, and the walls were white with the deadly whiteness of alabaster. A tiny altar, on which burnt the conventional three candles, fronted them as they entered, and the screen glittered with gold. A priest knelt before the altar, singing in a thin, cracked voice, so unmusically that the girl winced. Save for the priest and the party, the building was empty.

He rose at the sound of their footsteps, and stood waiting their approach. He was a young and singularly ugly man, and suspicion and fear were written plainly on his face.

"God save you, little brother of saints!" said Malinkoff.

"God save you, my son!" replied the priest mechanically. "What is it you want?"

"We need food and rest for this little lady, also hot coffee, and we will pay well."

Malinkoff knew that this latter argument was necessary. The priest shook his head.

"All the brethren have gone away from the monastery except Father Joachim, who is a timid man, Father Nicholas and myself," he said. "We have very little food and none to spare. They have eaten everything we had, and have killed my pretty chickens."

He did not say who "they" were, and Malinkoff was not sufficiently curious to inquire. He knew that the priests were no longer the power in the land that they were in the old days, and that there had been innumerable cases where the villagers had risen and slaughtered the men whose words hitherto had been as a law to them. A third of the monasteries in the Moscow Government had been sacked and burnt, and their congregations and officers dispersed.

He was surprised to find this beautiful chapel still intact, but he had not failed to notice the absence of the sacred vessels which usually adorned the altar, even in the midnight celebration.

"But can you do nothing for our little mama?" asked Malinkoff.

The priest shook his head.

"Our guests have taken everything," he said. "They have even turned Brother Joachim from the refectory."

"Your guests?" said Malinkoff.

The priest nodded.

"It is a great prince," he said in awe. "Terrible things are happening in the world, Antichrist is abroad, but we know little of such things in the monastery. The peasants have been naughty and have broken down our wall, slain our martyred brother Mathias—we could not find his body," he added quickly, "and Brother Joachim thinks that the Jews have eaten him so that by the consecrated holiness of his flesh they might avert their eternal damnation."

"Who is your prince?" asked Malcolm, hope springing in his breast.

There were still powerful factions in Russia which were grouped about the representatives and relatives of the late reigning house.

"I do not know his name," said the priest, "but I will lead you to him. Perhaps he has food."

He extinguished two of the candles on the altar, crossing himself all the while he was performing this ceremony, then led them through the screen and out at the back of the chapel. Malcolm thought he saw a face peering round the door as they approached it, and the shadow of a flying form crossing the dark yard. Possibly the timid Father Joachim he thought. Running along the wall was a low-roofed building.

"We are a simple order," said the priest, "and we live simply."

He had taken a candle lantern before he left the chapel, and this he held up to give them a better view. Narrow half-doors, the tops being absent, were set in the face of the building at intervals.

"Look!" he said, and pushed the lamp into the black void.

"A stable?" said Malinkoff.

He might have added: "a particularly draughty and unpleasant stable." There were straw-filled mangers and straw littered the floor.

"Do you keep many horses?"

The priest shook his head.

"Here we sleep," he said, "as directed in a vision granted to our most blessed saint and founder, St. Basil the Leper. For to him came an angel in the night, saying these words: 'Why sleepest thou in a fine bed when our Lord slept lowly in a stable?'"

He led the way across the yard to a larger building.

"His lordship may not wish to be disturbed, and if he is asleep I will not wake him."

"How long has he been here?" asked Malcolm.

"Since morning," repeated the other.

They were in a stone hall, and the priest hesitated. Then he opened the door cautiously, and peeped in. The room was well illuminated; they could see the hanging kerosene lamps from where they stood.

"Come," said the priest's voice in a whisper, "he is awake."

Malcolm went first. The room, though bare, looked bright and warm; a big wood fire blazed in an open hearth, and before it stood a man dressed in a long blue military coat, his hands thrust into his pockets. The hood of the coat was drawn over his head, and his attitude was one of contemplation. Malcolm approached him.

"Excellenz," he began, "we are travellers who desire——"

Slowly the man turned.

"Oh, you 'desire'!" he bellowed. "What do you desire, Comrade Hay? I will tell you what *I* desire—my beautiful little lamb, my pretty little wife!"

It was Boolba.

Chapter 19

The End of Boolba

Cherry Bim, the last of the party to enter the room, made a dash for the door, and came face to face with the levelled rifle held in the hands of a soldier who had evidently been waiting the summons of Boolba's shout. Behind him were three other men. Cherry dropped to the ground as the man's rifle went off, shooting as he fell, and the man tumbled down. Scrambling to his feet, he burst through the doorway like a human cannon ball, but not even his nimble guns could save him this time. The hall was full of soldiers, and they bore him down by sheer weight.

They dragged him into the refectory, bleeding, and the diversion at any rate had had one good effect. Only Boolba was there, roaring and raging, groping a swift way round the walls, one hand searching, the other guiding.

"Where are they?" he bellowed. "Come to me, my little beauty. Hay! I will burn alive. Where are they?"

"Little Commissary," said the leader of the soldiers, "she is not here. They did not pass out."

"Search, search!" shouted Boolba, striking at the man. "Search, you pig!"

"We have the other boorjoo," stammered the man.

"Search!" yelled Boolba. "There is a door near the fire—is it open?"

The door lay in the shadow, and the man ran to look.

"It is open, comrade," he said.

"After them, after them!"

Boolba howled the words, and in terror they left their prisoner and flocked out of the door. Cherry stood in the centre of the room, his hands strapped behind his back, his shirt half ripped from his body, and looked up into the big blinded face which came peering towards him as though, by an effort of will, it could glimpse his enemy.

"You are there?"

Boolba's hands passed lightly over the gun-man's face, fell upon his shoulders, slipped down the arm.

"Is this the thief? Yes, yes; this is the thief. What is he doing?"

He turned, not knowing that the soldiers had left him alone, and again his hands passed lightly over Cherry's face.

"This is good," he said, as he felt the bands on the wrists. "To-morrow, little brother, you will be dead."

He might have spared himself his exercise and his reproaches, because to Cherry Bim's untutored ear his reviling was a mere jabber of meaningless words. Cherry was looking round to find something sharp enough on which to cut the strap which bound him, but there was nothing that looked like a knife in the room. He knew he had a minute, and probably less, to make his escape. His eyes rested for a moment on the holster at Boolba's belt, and he side-stepped.

"Where are you going?"

Boolba's heavy hand rested on his shoulder.

"Not out of the doorway, my little pigeon. I am blind, but——"

So far he had got when Cherry turned in a flash, so that his back was toward Boolba. He stooped, and made a sudden dash backward, colliding with the Commissary, and in that second his hand had gripped the gun at Boolba's waist. There was a strap across the butt, but it broke with a jerk.

Then followed a duel without parallel. Boolba pulled his second gun and fired, and, shooting as blindly, Cherry fired backward. He heard a groan over his shoulder and saw Boolba fall to his knees. Then he ran for the main door, stumbled past the state-bedroom of the monks, and into the chapel. It was his one chance that the priest had returned to his devotions, and he found the man on his knees.

"Percy," said Cherry, "unfasten that strap."

The priest understood no language but his own. But a gesture, the strap about the wrists, blue and swollen, and the long revolver, needed no explanation. The strap fell off and Cherry rubbed his wrists.

He opened the breech of his gun; he had four shells left, but he was alone against at least twenty men. He guessed that Boolba had made the monastery his advance headquarters whilst he was waiting for news of the fugitives, and probably not twenty but two hundred were within call.

He reached the road and made for the place where the car had been left. If the others had escaped they also would go in that direction. He saw no guard or sentry, and heard no sound from the walled enclosure of the monastery. He struck against something in the roadway and stooped and picked it up. It was stitched in a canvas cover and it felt like a book. He suddenly remembered the scraps of conversation he had overheard between the girl and Malcolm.

This, then, was the "Book of All-Power."

"Foolishness," said Cherry, and put it in his pocket. But the book showed one thing clearly—the others had got away. He had marked the place where they had stopped, but the car was gone!

It was too dark to see the tracks, but there was no question that it had been here, for he found an empty petrol tin and the still air reeked of rubber solution.

He had need of all his philosophy. He was in an unknown country, a fugitive from justice, and that country was teeming with soldiers. Every road was watched, and he had four cartridges between him and capture. There was only one thing to do, and that was to go back the way the car had come, and he stepped out undauntedly, halting now and again to stoop and look along the railway line, for he was enough of an old campaigner to know how to secure a skyline.

Then in the distance he saw a regular line of lights, and those lights were moving. It was a railway train, and apparently it was turning a curve, for one by one the lights disappeared and only one flicker, which he judged was on the engine, was visible. He bent down again and saw the level horizon of a railway embankment less than two hundred yards on his left, and remembered that Malinkoff had spoken of the Warsaw line.

He ran at full speed, floundering into pools, breaking through bushes, and finally scrambled up the steep embankment. How to board the train seemed a problem which was insuperable, if the cars were moving at any speed. There was little foothold by the side of the track, and undoubtedly the train was moving quickly, for now the noise of it was a dull roar, and he, who was not wholly unacquainted with certain unauthorized forms of travel, could judge to within a mile an hour the rate it was travelling.

He fumbled in his pocket and found a match. There was no means of making a bonfire. The undergrowth was wet, and he had not so much as a piece of paper in his pocket.

"The book!"

He pulled it out, ripped off the canvas cover with his knife, and tried to open it. The book was locked, he discovered, but locks were to Cherry like pie-crusts—made to be broken. A wrench and the covers fell apart.

He tore out the first three or four pages, struck the match, and the flame was touching the corner of the paper when his eyes fell upon the printed words. He stood open-mouthed, the flame still burning, gazing at the torn leaf until the burning match touched his finger and he dropped it.

Torn between doubts, and dazed as he was, the train might have passed him, but the light of a match in the still, dark night could be seen for miles, and he heard the jar of the brakes. He pushed the book and the loose leaves into his pocket and ran along the embankment to meet the slowing special—for special it was.

He managed to pass the engine unnoticed, then, crouching down until the last carriage was abreast, he leapt up, caught the rail and swung himself on to the rear footboard, up the steel plates which serve as steps, to the roof of the carriage, just as the train stopped.

There were excited voices demanding explanations, there was a confusion of orders, and presently the train moved on, gathering speed, and Cherry had time to think. It was still dark when they ran into a little junction, and, peeping over the side, he saw a group of officers descend from a carriage to stretch their legs. To them came a voluble and gesticulating railway official, and again there was a confusion of voices. He was telling them something and his tone was apologetic, almost fearful. Then, to Cherry's amazement, he heard somebody speak in English. It was the voice of a stranger, a drawling English voice.

"Oh, I say! Let them come on, general! I wouldn't leave a dog in this country—really I wouldn't."

"But it is against all the rules of diplomacy," said a gruffer voice in the same language.

"Moses!" gasped Cherry.

The road led into the station-yard and he had seen the car. There was no doubt of it. The lights from one of the train windows were sufficiently strong to reveal it, and behind the stationmaster was another little group in the shadow.

"It is a matter of life and death." It was Malcolm's voice. "I must get this lady to the Polish frontier—it is an act of humanity I ask."

"English, eh?" said the man called the general. "Get on board."

Malcolm took the girl in his arms before them all.

"Go, darling," he said gently.

"I cannot go without you," she said, but he shook his head.

"Malinkoff and I must wait. We cannot leave Cherry. We are going back to find him. I am certain he has escaped."

"I will not leave without you," she said firmly.

"You'll all have to come or all have to stay," said the Englishman briskly. "We haven't any time to spare, and the train is now going on. You see," he said apologetically, "it isn't our train at all, it belongs to the Polish Commission, and we're only running the food end of the negotiations. We have been fixing up terms between the Red Army and the Poles, and it is very irregular that we should take refugees from the country at all."

"*Go!*"

Malcolm heard the hoarse whisper, and it was as much as he could do to stop himself looking up. He remembered the motor-car and Cherry's mysterious and providential appearance from the roof, and he could guess the rest.

"Very well, we will go. Come, Malinkoff, I will explain in the car," said Malcolm.

They lifted the girl into the carriage and the men followed. A shriek from the engine, a jerk of the cars, and the train moved on. Before the rear carriage had cleared the platform a car rocked into the station-yard, dashing through the frail wooden fencing on to the platform itself.

"*Stoi! Stoi!*"

Boolba stood up in the big touring car, his arms outstretched, the white bandage about his neck showing clearly in the car lights. Cherry Bim rose to his knees and steadied himself. Once, twice, three times he fired, and Boolba pitched over the side of the car dead.

"I had a feeling that we should meet again," said Cherry. "That's not a bad gun."

Chapter the Last

"All my life," said Cherry Bim, fondling his Derby hat affectionately, "I have been what is called by night-court reporters a human parricide."

He occupied a corner seat in the first-class compartment which had been placed at the disposal of the party. To the Peace Commissioners in their saloon the fugitives had no existence. Officially they were not on the train, and the hot meal which came back to them from the Commissioner's own kitchenette was officially sent to "extra train-men," and was entered as such on the books of the chef.

The girl smiled. There was cause for happiness, for these dreary flats which were passing the window were the flats of Poland.

"I have often thought, Mr. Bim, that you were a human angel!"

Cherry beamed.

"Why, that's what I was named after," he said. "Ain't you heard of the Cherry Bims? My sister Sarah was named the same way—you've heard of Sarah Bims?"

"Seraphims," laughed Malcolm; "true, it's near enough. But why this dissertation on your moral character, Cherry?"

"I'm only remarking," said Cherry, "I wouldn't like you gu—fellers to go away thinkin' that high-class female society hadn't brought about a change in what I would describe, for want of a better word, as my outlook."

"All our outlooks have been shaken up," said the girl, laying her hand on Cherry's arm.

"I am a Grand Duchess of Russia and you are—you are——"

"Yes, I'm that," said Cherry, helping her out. "I'm one of nature's extractors. But I'm through. I hate the idea of workin' and maybe I won't have to, because I've got enough of the—well, any way, I've got enough."

Malcolm slapped him on the knee.

"You've brought more from Russia than we have, Cherry," he said.

"But not the greatest prize." It was the silent Malinkoff who spoke. "Highness, is there no way of recovering your father's fortune?"

She shook her head.

"It is gone," she said quietly, "and if Russia were pacified to-morrow I should be poor—you know that, Malcolm!"

He nodded.

"I have not even," she smiled, "poor Israel Kensky's wonderful book."

"I was a careless fool," growled Malcolm, "when we struck the road I was so intent upon getting to the auto that I did not realize the book had dropped out. We hadn't a second to lose," he explained for the third time to Cherry. "The soldiers were searching in the yard when Malinkoff found the breach in the wall. I hated leaving you——"

"Aw!" said the disgusted Cherry. "Ain't we settled that? Didn't I hear you tellin' Percy—and say, is it true that the young lady is—is broke?"

"'Broke' is exactly the word," she said cheerfully. "I am going to be a nice Scottish wife and live within my husband's means—why, Cherry?"

He had a book in his hand—the "Book of All-Power."

"Where——?"

"Found it on the road," he said. "I broke the lock an' tore out a couple of leaves to light a flare. I wanted to flag the train—but I've got 'em—the leaves, I mean."

"You found it?"

She reached out her hand for the volume, but he did not give it to her.

"I can't read Russian," he said. "What does this say?" and he pointed to the inscription on the cover, and she read, translating as she went on:

"The Book of All-Power

Herein is the magic of power and the words and symbols which unlock the sealed hearts of men and turn their proud wills to water."

Cherry was silent.

"That's a lie," he said quietly, "for it didn't turn my will to water—take it, miss!"

She took it from his hand, wondering, and turned the broken cover. She could not believe her eyes. . . and turned the leaves quickly. Every page was a Bank of England note worth a thousand pounds.

"THAT WAS HOW KENSKY KEPT his money evidently," said Malinkoff. "In such troublesome times as the Jews passed through, he must have thought it safest to convert his property into English money, and when he had reached the limit of his hoard he bound the notes into a book."

The girl turned her bewildered face to Cherry. "Did you know that this was money?" she asked. "Sure," he said; "didn't I start in to burn it?"

THE END

A Note About the Author

Edgar Wallace (1875–1932) was a London-born writer who rose to prominence during the early twentieth century. With a background in journalism, he excelled at crime fiction with a series of detective thrillers following characters J.G. Reeder and Detective Sgt. (Inspector) Elk. Wallace is known for his extensive literary work, which has been adapted across multiple mediums, including over 160 films. His most notable contribution to cinema was the novelization and early screenplay for 1933's *King Kong*.

A Note from the Publisher

Spanning many genres, from non-fiction essays to literature classics to children's books and lyric poetry, Mint Edition books showcase the master works of our time in a modern new package. The text is freshly typeset, is clean and easy to read, and features a new note about the author in each volume. Many books also include exclusive new introductory material. Every book boasts a striking new cover, which makes it as appropriate for collecting as it is for gift giving. Mint Edition books are only printed when a reader orders them, so natural resources are not wasted. We're proud that our books are never manufactured in excess and exist only in the exact quantity they need to be read and enjoyed.

bookfinity™

Discover more of your favorite classics with Bookfinity™.

- Track your reading with custom book lists.
- Get great book recommendations for your personalized Reader Type.
- Add reviews for your favorite books.
- AND MUCH MORE!

Visit **bookfinity.com** and take the fun Reader Type quiz to get started.

Enjoy our classic and modern companion pairings!

Printed in the USA
CPSIA information can be obtained
at www.ICGtesting.com
JSHW082147140824
68134JS00002B/26